Princ...

...unexpectedly leads to their happy-ever-after!

Princesses Isabella and Francesca of Monterossa
have always been inseparable—until now! As the
king's health falters, their lives stand on the brink of
irrevocable change, with Francesca's ascension to
the throne drawing nearer. So when the twins find
themselves in London for an official engagement,
they decide to embrace one final adventure before
surrendering to royal duty...

Only, Isabella stumbles upon her billionaire ex-fiancé,
Rowan—and he's even more handsome than she
remembers. But when they're caught in a misleadingly
intimate moment, they have no choice but to chase
the overzealous paparazzi into the city streets!

In *How to Win Back a Royal*
by Justine Lewis

And with her free-spirited sister gallivanting around
London, Francesca enlists the help of her
royal protection officer to track Isabella down.
The very same bodyguard she's been harboring
very off-limits feelings for!

In *Temptation in a Tiara*
by Karin Baine

Both available now!

Dear Reader,

In news that will surprise no one, I am a big fan of the television series *The Crown*. I loved the episode in the final season depicting the night of VE Day when the Princesses Elizabeth and Margaret went out incognito in London, a story that has always intrigued me.

When my editor asked if I would like to write a royal rom-com duet with the wonderful Karin Baine, I jumped at the chance. We had plenty of ideas, but when I mentioned this story, Karin's eyes lit up and it was settled.

We took this as our starting point and dreamed up twin sisters Francesca and Isabella, who give their bodyguards the slip to have incognito adventures one night in modern-day London.

Unfortunately (or fortunately) for Isabella, she runs into her ex—the handsome, brilliant Rowan James, the man who broke her heart when he called off their engagement days before their wedding.

I hope you enjoy Rowan and Isabella's story—and remember to check out Francesca's story as well (if you haven't already).

Justine

xx

HOW TO WIN BACK A ROYAL

JUSTINE LEWIS

ROMANCE

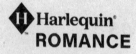

Harlequin®
ROMANCE

ISBN-13: 978-1-335-21637-3

How to Win Back a Royal

Recycling programs for this product may not exist in your area.

Harlequin Enterprises ULC
22 Adelaide St. West, 41st Floor
Toronto, Ontario M5H 4E3, Canada
www.Harlequin.com

Printed in U.S.A.

Justine Lewis writes uplifting, heartwarming contemporary romances. She lives in Australia with her hero husband, two teenagers and an outgoing puppy. When she isn't writing, she loves to walk her dog in the bush near her house, attempt to keep her garden alive and search for the perfect frock. She loves hearing from readers, and you can visit her at justinelewis.com.

For Peter. Again. Because he makes me laugh
more than anyone else in the world.

Praise for
Justine Lewis

CHAPTER ONE

'WHAT'S NEXT ON the schedule?' Isabella di Marzano, Princess of Monterossa, kicked off her red designer Italian pumps and lifted her bare feet onto the plush sofa. She leant her head back and groaned. Her feet hurt, her head ached and now she was alone with just her twin sister Francesca for company, she could no longer ignore the tightness in her chest that had been with her on and off for the past few weeks. Worry. An ever-present, persistent worry, lurking at the back of her mind like an intruder ready to pounce.

The last year had been Isabella's own *annus horribilis*: first the abrupt end of her engagement and now her father's illness. A skin cancer diagnosis that had shocked everyone. King Leonardo was in his early sixties and they'd thought he was fit, but a routine examination had discovered not one, but two melanomas that had already spread to his lymph nodes.

Isabella desperately hoped her sister's answer would be 'Nothing,' and that she could run a hot steamy bath and submerge herself in bubbles and fragrant oils, but that was rarely the case these days. Ever since their father had become ill, she and Francesca had increased their already busy schedule of public engagements and private duties to ease the pressure on her parents.

'Mother's coming to talk to us about London,' Francesca said.

Isabella sat up straight at that. *This* was a public engagement she'd been looking forward to, despite everything going on. She had a plan. And it wasn't the plan her mother was about to talk to them about.

In a few days she and Francesca would travel to London for the coronation of the new British King. With their father still in hospital and their mother wanting to stay with him, Francesca and Isabella, the twin princesses of Monterossa, would attend and represent their parents. It would be one of the largest events either princess had ever attended, with many reigning monarchs and heads of state from across the world attending.

Isabella knew some of the guests going, was distantly related to several, but many she knew only by sight. From the magazines and newspapers, just like anybody else. An event like this would be a dress rehearsal for the real thing. The life that awaited her older sister.

Born on the same day, at the same hour, yet five crucial minutes apart, the Princesses were destined for different lives. Despite this, or maybe because of it, their parents had insisted the girls be brought up and educated together. Isabella had essentially been trained for a job she'd never have. Her parents explained that Isabella's role was to support her sister. They insisted that being her sister's best friend and closest adviser was a valid job description, though Isabella wasn't so sure. So far, for the first twenty-nine years of their lives it hadn't mattered too much. They came as a pair of princesses. Two for the price of one.

But all that might soon be about to change.

Two months ago her father had undergone surgery to remove the cancers, but his recovery had been slow, with more complications than anticipated. After commencing immunotherapy he had developed an infection, necessitating return to hospital, where he remained to continue his treatment. At first Isabella had tried to tell herself it was a precaution—he was the King after all and everyone was being particularly cautious—but as the weeks and a further surgery went by, she no longer knew whether to believe the doctors' assurances. Isabella had been reading everything she could about skin cancer, its causes and treatments. She could hardly believe that, living in a sun-soaked Mediterranean country as they were, they had all been so nonchalant about the risks. Isabella was beginning to wonder if this new state of affairs, with her sister carrying out the bulk of the royal duties, would soon become permanent.

She usually discussed everything with Francesca, but this was different. This wasn't just their father's health—which was worrying enough—it was the one thing that would change their close bond as nothing else would.

There could only ever be one queen, and that would be Francesca.

Francesca stood up straight, flicking efficiently through something on her phone. Isabella had no doubt Francesca would make a wonderful monarch—that was not what worried her. What worried her was how Francesca becoming queen would change their relationship, because surely it would.

Francesca was everything a monarch should be: dedicated, poised, intelligent. In comparison, Isabella often felt like the support act or a trusty sidekick. She tried not to be the comedic relief in the story that was Francesca's life, but it was hard when the press expected her to take on the role of 'the irresponsible spare' or 'the playgirl princess'. Isabella was neither of those things. She was as serious about representing her country as her sister.

A quick knock at the door announced the Queen's arrival. She swept into the room and studied them both briefly, taking in Isabella's bare feet on the sofa, Francesca's flawless appearance.

She didn't say anything, but she didn't have to. Every expression on their mother's face told an entire story. She was, by training, an actress. A qualification that had been particularly useful to a queen over the years. Being able to feign delight or surprise and smile on demand was particularly useful now when her daughters both knew that what she really wanted to do was crumble with stress.

'Thank you both again for going to London on our behalf,' Queen Gloria said.

'Of course, you know we'll do anything to help you,' Francesca said.

'I know, but I want you both to know that we do appreciate it very much. It's going to be an exhausting visit.'

'How so?' Isabella imagined she'd be sitting down in the abbey for much of the time. Attend a few parties, but these sorts of parties were never debaucherous all-nighters. She'd be expected to sit on the one glass of champagne all night and be home in bed by midnight.

The Queen talked them through their schedule for the day of the coronation: wake at five a.m. Five a.m.! Breakfast, hair and make-up before they were picked up from their hotel at seven. A car would take them to one of the gathering points where they would get on a coach with the other dignitaries.

There would be no pulling up outside the abbey

in their own car or carriage for them, or for most of the guests—royalty, politicians, and celebrities. Most guests would be shipped to and from the abbey in large buses. They would arrive several hours before the ceremony to ensure everyone and everything was in place and afterwards they would be collected the same way.

'I'd watch how much you drink. You'll be sitting in the abbey for close to six hours with no bathroom breaks.'

Francesca looked at Isabella and said, 'And they think being a princess is glamorous.'

They both laughed. Being a princess was often very much the opposite of glamorous. Eating fermented Baltic sea herring on an official trip to Sweden, standing in high heels for hours at a time, often in the sun. Having your private life spoken about and analysed by the rest of the world.

Their mother shook her head with an exasperated sigh. Representing your country was an honour and a privilege that outweighed the downsides was what she would've told them, if she hadn't already told them that weekly for their entire lives.

Isabella *knew* it was an honour and she loved supporting her sister and her parents, but glamour, she thought, was not all it was advertised to be.

After six hours in Westminster Abbey, with no food or toilet breaks, they would attend a late lunch stand-up reception at the palace with the new King and other important guests.

'At least the food is good at the palace,' Francesca said, and they both nodded, remembering a particularly nice dinner they had all once enjoyed hosted by the former King. 'Do you remember the chocolate and praline ice cream?' The sisters groaned with delight at the memory of that dessert.

Their mother shook her head again. 'After that, you'll have time to get dressed for the official function that evening. The King isn't hosting anything, there are too many dignitaries in town for an official state dinner, but the new Duke of Oxford will host a private party at the Ashton. A private club in Mayfair, not far from the palace.

'We understand the King and Queen may attend the event at the Ashton, though won't be the official hosts. And who can blame them? They'll have had an exhausting day. Barbier will come tomorrow to arrange your outfits for the coronation and the party afterwards.'

Isabella tried to hide her grimace. Christian Barbier was her mother's favourite stylist, but his recommendations tended to make both princesses look older than how Isabella preferred to dress. She preferred younger designers, more contemporary styles, outfits she had put together herself, but this was not a fight she wanted to have with her mother right now.

Not this week.

And maybe not this year.

'And I've sent you both something. A special file. That I'd like you to keep confidential.'

The sisters exchanged a look. As princesses and one and two in line to the throne they were sometimes trusted with classified information, but it was shown to them by their father or the government. Not their mother.

'What is it?' Francesca asked.

'I've put together a list.'

'Yes?'

'Of some of the guests attending the coronation and the party.'

Isabella closed her eyes. She had a horrible feeling what her mother was going to say next.

While neither the King nor the Queen would ever dictate who their daughters should marry, they did have firm ideas on the *sort* of man who would make a suitable life partner for both their daughters. Someone who was prepared to put Monterossa first. Someone who understood a princess's role and duties. Someone who wasn't easily spooked by public attention. All specific criteria added after the abrupt end of Isabella's engagement last summer.

'There are some photos and biographies.'

'Of men?' Francesca guessed.

'Single men. Eligible single men.'

Francesca turned to Isabella and they shared a look of sympathy and commiseration. Francesca had her own failed engagement in her past as well. Benigno, a duke, had called off his engagement to Francesca, but, unlike Isabella's reaction to her broken engagement, Francesca seemed more relieved by this than anything. Isabella was too, if she was honest. While her parents thought Benigno was perfect for Francesca, Isabella knew they didn't love one another.

Unlike her and Rowan.

'It's not that I don't trust you, it's just that, as we've said, we know it will be easier if you find a man who's from our world, or who at least has an understanding of it. Its responsibilities.' The Queen turned to Isabella. 'And its pitfalls and hazards.'

Isabella looked down, unable to meet anyone's eye.

'I'm not trying to tell you who to choose, but I don't want to see either of you hurt again. The men in this file are men with similar backgrounds, like-minded values, but also with compatible expectations.'

'Mother, is this really the time for either of us to be dating?' Francesca said.

Isabella knew exactly what her mother was trying to do—steer them in the direction of men from their own class, so that neither of them faced the Rowan situation again. Isabella also knew that, in her own way, her sister was trying to defend her and even Rowan. The man who had broken off their engagement three days before their wedding last summer.

She didn't hate him, which was a pity. It might be easier if she hated him, but she couldn't even despise him for his timing. It wasn't until a week before the wedding date that the truly vile headlines had come out, calling him a social climber, a gold-digger…neither of which were even true. Rowan had a larger fortune than Isabella would inherit, several times over. One he had made on his own.

Instead of hate, what was left was simply grief. And the knowledge that there never would be a man she could ever trust again with her heart. She was a princess, she had to avoid gossip and scandal of any kind. The last two men who had become engaged to Monterossa's princesses had broken off those engagements, leaving a mountain of headlines and gossip in their wake. So Isabella was hardly about to race to the altar with anyone at the moment— whether he was on her mother's list or not.

'I'm simply suggesting you consider who you might speak to at the celebrations, that's all. I'm asking you—imploring you—to keep the file secret. It's information only, nothing more,' the Queen said.

Francesca rolled her eyes in Isabella's direction, but so their mother couldn't see.

A timely idea and a passion had helped Rowan James, a working-class boy from South East London, make his first billion. His brilliant business skills had helped him make the next five. Barely into his twenties he had launched the first of what was to be a whole suite of apps supporting mental health, with guided meditations, breathing and mindfulness exercises, and plenty more besides. He had designed one specifically for eating disorders, another for addiction and, as Isabella had recently read, he would soon be launching one for teenagers. He was in demand for so many reasons and his business was growing stronger each year. He had had no problem relocating to New York after their failed relationship. She couldn't even blame him for leaving her, not when the press had been so cruel. She wouldn't wish that sort of attention on anyone she cared for.

Her family had never disapproved of Rowan. Like Isabella, they had also thought that he was her perfect match, but it turned out they had all been living in their own bubble and hadn't anticipated the interest the world's media would take in them or the ferocity of that interest. The press had hounded Rowan, and when that had yielded no attention-grabbing headlines, they had gone after his family. His brother, but most of all Rowan's father.

Right now, particularly with her father's illness, Isabella had no plans to date anyone, let alone get married. Maybe she never would, and that was fine. All she wanted to do in the immediate future was let her hair down a little. Have some fun and for a few precious moments forget everything that was happening with her father. And Rowan.

So she didn't open the file with her mother's list. Instead, she flicked over the pages of the itinerary. It was called 'A celebration' but it certainly wasn't going to be a relaxing party. It was a strictly choreographed event. Each minute accounted for, down to the one allocated toilet break. It was an appearance. Good practice for the next coronation they had to attend. One at which one of them might be a participant, not just a guest.

No. Isabella refused to even think about that. It would be years away.

Not if Father abdicates.

It was a matter she'd thought she'd overheard her parents discussing before she'd entered his hospital room last week. She'd caught her mother saying, 'You can't do anything without discussing it with Francesca.'

'And Isabella?' the King had said.

'No. Not yet.'

Isabella's heart had sunk when she'd heard those words. The first fracturing. A recognition that she and her sister were not equals, were not destined to follow the same path.

Isabella had slipped away, gone to the bathroom to press a cold towel to her burning face, before returning to the hospital room, this time announcing her arrival with a loud knock. There had been no mention of abdication or anything like it since then, and Isabella hadn't mentioned what she had heard to Francesca.

'No one in this room is getting any younger,' the Queen added. 'You're both approaching thirty.' She said this often, as though it were some kind of cut-off date, but that didn't stop irritation rising in Isabella's chest.

You weren't raised a royal! Isabella wanted to retort. Her mother, who had been born and raised in the United States and been a successful actress, didn't know the first thing about being a queen when she met Leonardo. Though she had been accustomed to being in the public eye, which probably had helped, as had the fact that she had married before the advent of the Internet and social media.

Looking from one daughter to the other and their stricken expressions, Gloria softened her expression and said, 'Love never comes on time.'

'Is that a song lyric? Are you quoting pop music at us?'

'And what if I am? My point is that love comes around when it does, never at the perfect time.' The Queen picked up her things. 'Anyway, I'm going back to the hospital.'

'Send Dad our love,' Francesca and Isabella replied.

When their mother had left, Isabella fell back onto the couch.

'Argh! Isn't there enough pressure on us going to this thing? Now she wants us to bring an eligible man back.' She groaned.

'She just wants us to be happy,' Francesca said.

'I know.'

'You especially.'

Isabella ground her teeth together. Realised what she was doing and rubbed her jaw. The break-up with Rowan had crushed her, as her sister was well aware. Isabella didn't want to dwell on those dark weeks and months; she needed to look forward.

'I have an idea about London. And it doesn't involve Mother's list.'

Francesca raised one of her perfect dark eyebrows.

'I think we should sneak out of the party and go and do something on our own.'

Francesca laughed. 'We can't do that.'

'Why not?'

'It's an official engagement—we're representing not only our parents but also the country. Besides, it's at an exclusive club. Where else in London would be better than that?'

Just about anywhere, Isabella wanted to mutter.

'Leanne is having a party.' Leanne was a singer and friend of Isabella's.

Francesca laughed. 'We really can't go there. Too many people we know would see us.'

It was a good point. 'Okay then, just to a normal bar, where regular people are.'

'There will be eligible men at the Duke's party,' Francesca said.

'Name one.'

They both opened up their mother's list. It wasn't long. There were some aristocrats, some other royals they already knew. The pool of young royals and aristocrats in Europe was hardly deep and they both knew it.

'We've met most of these guys before.'

'The Earl of Hereford?'

'Gay.'

'The Count of Westphalia?'

'The one who grabbed my arse at our father's jubilee?'

Francesca groaned.

At least she's thinking about it though. She hasn't dismissed the idea of sneaking away outright.

'I can't date an ordinary person,' Francesca said.

'Ordinary? I'm not suggesting you date an ordinary person. I'm suggesting you find an *extraordinary* one who doesn't happen to be titled and at the stuffy Duke's stuffy ball.'

'Someone who is already in the public eye, someone who understands our world would be a better match. Like Mother was.'

The romance between their father, a prince,

and their mother, the beautiful actress, had been called a fairy-tale romance. For the twins, their parents' marriage was the gold standard of relationships. Their parents still adored one another deeply and passionately after over thirty years. Their father's ill health had hit their mother hard.

Francesca and the Queen did have a point; someone who understood the pressures was less likely to freak out at the circus that came with dating a princess. As Rowan had.

But Isabella's intention wasn't for either of them to meet someone in London. Isabella wasn't about to make the same mistake she had with Rowan, rushing into a serious relationship before either of them were ready, and definitely not pushing someone into it, as she had with Rowan. All she wanted was a few moments of freedom. Of being out, alone with her sister, pretending they were regular people. Forgetting their responsibilities, the weight of other current stressors for a few hours. It was a whirlwind trip away from Monterossa, just forty-eight hours. She wanted them both to make the most of it.

'Could we do both? We need to go to the Duke's party for a while at least,' Francesca asked.

Isabella knew she was wavering. Now to reel her in with her plan.

'Sure, we put in an appearance at the Duke's party and then slip out to the real world.'

'Mother will know if we leave early.'

'No, she won't. We'll sneak out the back. No one will know. Don't you ever want to do something *you* want to do? Be spontaneous? Step outside your comfort zone?'

Francesca looked down.

'I don't have the luxury of being spontaneous. I don't wish for things I can't have. It's counterproductive.'

Isabella felt a moment of pity. It was just as well she was the spare, not the heir. She chafed against her royal status in a way her dutiful older sister didn't.

'You don't have to be sensible all the time, you know.'

'Yes, I do.'

'Okay, maybe most of the time, but can't this be the one per cent of the time when you aren't?'

She nearly had her.

'You're probably going to be married soon,' Isabella said, trying her winning argument.

'I'm no closer to getting married than you are.'

'Yes, you are. You just need to find the right person. And believe me, he's not on Mother's list.'

Francesca rolled her eyes.

'We may not be about to be married but things might be about to change,' Isabella whispered, even though no one could hear except the palace walls. It didn't do to say things like 'Father might be about to die and you'll be the Queen,' too loudly.

'You don't know that.'

'No, but we both know they will one day. It might be sooner than we thought. This could be your last chance to go somewhere we're not recognised.'

'They still recognise us in London.'

Isabella looked at her beautiful sister and had to agree; no disguise in the world could hide her gorgeousness. Francesca had inherited her mother's sultry movie star good looks. She had long dark hair that flowed in thick, shiny tresses and flawless skin.

The twins were fraternal and while Isabella knew she was attractive, she also knew she wasn't quite in her sister's league, and that was perfectly fine.

'Yes, but not as much as here. Besides, there'll be millions of people in London this weekend. Hundreds of other royals, celebrities. No one's going to notice a couple of princesses from a rock in the Mediterranean.'

Isabella received another glare. While the palace they lived in was technically on a large rocky island—the Gibraltar of the East, it was sometimes called—the kingdom of Monterossa was comprised of a group of islands and a chunk of mainland Italy's heel as well.

Francesca hated it when she called Monterossa a rock. Which was why Isabella did it.

'What if something happens?'

'What's going to happen? The streets will be teeming with police and security.'

'What if we get separated?'

Isabella took her sister's hand and squeezed. 'Not us. Never.'

CHAPTER TWO

ROWAN JAMES HAD lived in London most of his thirty-five years, but he'd never seen it look as it did today. The rain that had threatened to overshadow the coronation early that morning had cleared, leaving only occasional puddles that reflected the lights and added to the sparkle of the city.

The city where Isabella di Marzano was currently walking and breathing. Though, not this part of the city. The other part. The part on the other side of the river with the royals and the coronation guests.

Rowan was in his part of London. On the other side of the Thames. Though, granted, he was in a pretty nice bar, called Twilight, with some of his oldest friends. Celebrating what should have been a momentous night for his brother, Will, but it was only bringing back memories of Rowan's own pre-wedding celebration. An evening that had not ended well.

Rowan rubbed his chin, still not used to the

beard he was currently wearing. He'd grown it through the itchy stage and it was now reasonably thick. He only hoped it would do a good enough job of making him slightly unrecognisable. His plan—or, perhaps, hope—was to slip into the country for a bit without anyone but his family and friends realising.

Will noticed. 'What's with the beard?'

'They're fashionable.'

Will raised his eyebrow. 'When have you ever cared what's fashionable?'

'Okay, laziness.'

'Again, that's not you at all. The man who came up with the idea of MindER when he was just eighteen and turned that idea into a multimillion-dollar business? Single-minded? Yes. Stubborn. Definitely. Lazy? Not a bit.'

Rowan let his brother's gentle ribbing wash over him. He didn't want Will to know the real reason for the beard, the real cowardly reason. It was better that way.

Better for whom?

For Rowan, for starters. He was only on this side of the Atlantic for a week. Will's wedding was next weekend. Tonight was an informal night out for friends who had travelled to London for the wedding. It was definitely *not* a stag night; they were all being careful not to call it that after the disaster that had been Rowan's.

Last year, Will had thrown Rowan a pre-wedding party over a weekend in Paris but it had been crashed by a group of women. Women who had turned out to be hired by a tabloid. Rowan had been oblivious to the women's presence, talking to a friend, when a woman had come up next to him. Rowan had tried to leave, but it had been the image of him trying to push past her that had looked like an embrace that had been published. Rowan had been able to see she was wearing a skimpy top that was the colour of her skin but the subsequent photos had made her look topless. Will and his friends had been similarly caught. Nothing untoward had happened but the photos had made it look as if it were about to. The palace of Monterossa had come down hard on the paper, also feeling guilty they hadn't thought to send a palace official with Rowan, but that hardly mattered. Rowan was a fool for not having anticipated something like that himself.

His friends had suffered unacceptable stress and heartache. Relationships had almost been destroyed. Everyone's trust had been shaken. That, on top of the number the media had done on his family, exposing their lives and secrets, had been too much. He'd had to step away. He had loved Isabella deeply, but he couldn't put his family and friends through what the sharks of the tabloids had been doing to them.

Now, Rowan was about to launch his newest app, one designed specifically to help teenagers manage their mental health. For some businesses media attention was a good thing. Not in Rowan's case. He'd designed and built a suite of applications to support mental health, so photos of him with scantily clad women the week before his wedding, however innocent, did not help business. He couldn't be seen as a playboy. The untrue allegations that he, his friends and colleagues had partied excessively and engaged prostitutes had damaged their brand. Not to mention their personal relationships.

Apart from visiting his family, seeing a few close and trusted friends, and tonight, Rowan intended to spend the week in his hotel suite working on the launch of MindER. Immediately after the wedding he would travel back to New York. The beard, as pathetic as it was, would hopefully help him slip under the radar a little.

Rowan had no intention of upstaging Will and Lucy on their big day. And if his photo was taken in London he almost certainly would.

Rowan had lived in New York for less than a year, but he loved the way he felt anonymous. It wasn't so much that no one knew who he was, it was just that, with so many people even more famous than he was for far more scandalous things, no one really cared that he was Rowan James, Princess Dumper. They also forgot that he was a school dropout and an alleged gold-digging social climber.

The press attention given to Monterossa was nowhere near as febrile as that reserved for the British royal family, but it was greater than he'd first believed. Monterossa was a small but glamorous kingdom that had attracted worldwide notice thirty years ago when its handsome prince had married Hollywood royalty, the current Queen Gloria. The then prince and princess had produced beautiful twin daughters, Francesca and Isabella, and the world had been similarly captivated.

Isabella had been born into a fairy tale and he had grossly underestimated the attention that would bring to him. He'd been foolish enough to believe that the attention would be a good thing. Good for his business, for raising awareness of mental health. He couldn't believe how naive the Rowan James of two years ago had been.

Following their engagement, the tabloids had made his childhood sound positively Dickensian, implying his parents had been neglectful and that he'd practically been raised on the streets. They twisted stories about both his parents, reporting that his mother was a cocktail waitress when in truth she was the manager of a local pub. Worse than that, they had lapped up his father's past. Rowan's father had done time in his early twenties for dealing a small quantity of heroin. The dealing had been to support his own habit, a habit he'd kicked successfully while in prison.

Rowan's father had gone on to have a long and well-regarded career as a social worker, helping people who suffered the same problems that he had, and Rowan had had a secure and comfortable childhood. Far from being the pauper described by the papers, he had been better off than many people he knew.

But of course, the headlines never told you about life's complexities. You couldn't explain things like this in two hundred and eighty characters.

One thing that was undeniably true, though, was that his childhood had not been like Isabella's.

A beautiful princess, she'd walked straight out of a fairy-tale kingdom and into the bar where he'd been sitting at a global mental health summit he'd attended in Geneva two summers ago. He'd been relaxing after giving a successful talk about the development of MindER.

Rowan had never been a good student. While he'd liked the social aspect of school, he often had difficulties concentrating and sitting still. The only thing that could make him concentrate for long periods of time was computer gaming, a hobby that both his parents discouraged and which led to an endless cycle of arguments. They insisted he was intelligent, but the further Rowan fell behind at school, the less he believed this. He left school early when his English teacher suggested that there was little point in him continuing and picked up casual work in the pub in which his mother ran. He was lost, a failure, and made to feel bad about the one thing in the world he really enjoyed. Gaming.

When Rowan was a teenager, smart phones were beginning to become commonplace. With his knowledge of gaming and coding, he began to think of ways in which apps could be used and developed a few basic games. At the same time, his father, a life-long smoker, had been trying to quit and Rowan decided to see if he could develop a game to help him. With some basic coding knowledge, he developed an app to distract smokers with games and track days without cigarettes.

His father used it and recommended it to some friends and Rowan began to spend more and more time working on the game, which was how, to begin with, he thought of it. He roped in some friends who knew more about coding than he did and came up with a plan. It became, over time, MindER, which now had a suite of applications to support various aspects of mental health, guided meditation, mindfulness, sleep, exercises, movement and even dance. In two weeks they were launching their newest product, an app especially designed for young teenagers.

It had been a steep learning curve; he'd had to learn about coding, psychology and most of all how to run a multimillion-dollar business. But he'd been lucky. Lucky to have the right idea at the right time. Lucky to secure an investor. Lucky enough not to make any bad deals. Lucky to expand the business at just the right rate, not so quickly that he overstretched. Not so slow that he didn't capitalise on the need for the services his app delivered. Lucky that this was something that a school dropout could manage to do.

He'd been lucky.

And catching Isabella's eye in the bar of that Geneva hotel had been similarly lucky. She had wandered in with her sister, two discreet body-guards in tow, and he'd happened to look up at exactly the right moment.

She was beautiful.

Heart-in-your-throat-type beautiful. See-her-face-behind-your-closed-eyelids-overnight-type beautiful.

Plus she was confident. And he liked that. It was sexy as hell. It made him confident too. She wasn't afraid of sitting down next to him at the bar and asking what had brought him to Geneva. Despite his success, Rowan generally kept a low profile, which was difficult when you had a business to promote, but he preferred to let the product speak for itself. MindER was the brand, not him. They hadn't talked about their backgrounds, but about their passions, their dreams, things so utterly unconnected to real-life problems that it wasn't until several hours into the conversation—

when he was already half in love with her—that she told him she was a princess. By then it was too late.

Buoyed by the success of the talk he'd given at the summit, he'd been brave that evening too. Brave enough to ask her for another drink, brave enough to ask for her number. Brave enough to keep messaging her.

She saw him. She understood him. Despite their different upbringings, they understood one another. And that made him brave and her confident.

But then the bubble had burst, and she hadn't in fact been confident enough for both of them. And he had not been brave enough at all.

You made the right decision.

He knew that. He absolutely knew that.

Isabella knew it too.

In fact, the whole world knew a dropout like him didn't belong with a princess. The only one who hadn't caught up with the news was his stupid heart.

It was probably knowing she was in London tonight that brought thoughts of Isabella back to mind. Who was he kidding? She was never very far from his thoughts. Despite doing his best to erase her from his consciousness by working fourteen-hour days, making endless visits to the gym, swimming countless laps of the pool, it was all futile. It still didn't allow him to sleep at night and not lie awake thinking of her.

Sleep brought its own problems though. When his thoughts were untethered from consciousness he would dream about her. Dream she was in his arms. In his bed. Dream she was standing two metres away from him in a bar in London.

Rowan stepped back, into the shadow of the group of men standing next to him. He took several deep, even breaths. He was delirious. Losing what remained of his sanity. Isabella di Marzano, Princess of Monterossa was not in this South London bar.

He leant forward just a fraction.

Except, yes…yes, she really was.

Isabella stood alone off to the side of the bar, glancing occasionally at her phone, trying not to look as though she'd been abandoned by her sister.

She leant against the barrier at the edge of the leafy rooftop bar, Twilight, which afforded her a view over the edge of the building and the city. The sun had just set and the lights across London sparkled. The crowd circled around her. Behind the expansive bar, hundreds of brightly coloured bottles were stacked and under the lights glowed like gems. The music was fast, with an invigorating beat. After another drink or so she might be able to convince Francesca to find a dance floor.

Isabella had slipped off her jacket and draped

it over her arm. She wore a fitted red dress that stopped just above her ankles. The scooped neckline and thin straps allowed her bare skin to luxuriate in the warm evening air. With the jacket she looked elegant and formal enough for the official party, without the jacket she looked classy, but not overdressed for this upmarket bar.

Francesca was chatting to a man she'd spied at the bar. She was laughing and the man looked captivated, as well he might. It was good to be around people but with no one looking at her for a change. No one watching her every move, judging every innocent remark. The lack of scrutiny and pressure made Isabella feel lighter. Almost untethered. She hadn't yet decided whether that was a good thing or not. All her life she felt the tension between staying calm, keeping every emotion inside her contained and letting them all go. The two forces fighting against one another, tonight she was struggling to keep her feet on the ground.

This is the plan, remember? A night out as ordinary people before whatever happens is going to happen. She wanted Francesca to have fun. One last hurrah. Heck, *she* wanted to have some fun. That was the point of sneaking out of the Duke's party and going to a random bar in South London. The plan had also been to leave their bodyguards behind as well, except somehow Gallo had caught wind of their plan and made them agree to him coming along. He was, however, a discreet distance away, glaring at everyone in the bar in that way he had.

Despite standing here alone looking like a wall-flower she didn't have the slightest regret. Her sister looked happy as she flirted with the stranger. Isabella looked around the room at the groups of friends enjoying a night out, breathed in the warm air of the summer evening and the mood of optimism that had settled over the city.

She turned her gaze to the other side of the bar. There was a group of men, all tall, broad shouldered. They were dressed casually, as though they'd come from a football match. They were acting like friends who had not seen one another in some time. She tried to listen in without wanting to be too conspicuous. Then one of the men stood and turned to one side, revealing another man. And he was frowning.

It was a face she knew well. One that was tattooed on her heart.

She recognised the frown, the narrowing of his light brown eyes and the sudden tenseness in his shoulders. But there were differences as well. The beard for starters. Auburn, like the rest of his hair, thick and well established. It was clipped neatly and well groomed. Not the result of neglect, but purposeful.

He *wanted* to look different.

She didn't blame him one bit. She'd often toyed

with the idea of dying her own light brown hair to see if she'd be able to go unrecognised.

Beard or no beard, she'd recognise this man anywhere.

Why here? Why now? Why him? This was her 'get out there and forget Rowan James' weekend. This was *not* meant to be her 'run into your ex unexpectedly' weekend.

They were separated by two metres but an ocean of grief and pain. She stepped towards him, half wondering if he would simply turn and flee. She wouldn't blame him if he did. Her instincts told her to do the same.

But he moved in her direction as well, always the gentlemen, ever polite. He wouldn't have changed fundamentally in the eleven months since they had last seen one other.

'Rowan,' she said, her voice lilting embarrassingly upwards.

'Your Highness.'

She flinched at the title, one he had never ever called her by previously. He was wearing a fitted blue collared shirt that set off his beautiful eyes, and dark trousers. She hugged her own jacket tighter.

Should they kiss on the cheek? Shake hands? Or just continue to shift awkwardly from foot to foot as she was doing now?

Rowan was less hesitant than she and bent down the half-foot in height necessary to kiss her lightly. As his rough cheek brushed against hers she caught his familiar cologne, high notes of citrus, heart notes of desire and bass notes of heartbreak.

Her olfactory memories jolted everything to the front of her mind. Their first serendipitous meeting in Geneva, short and chaste, followed by several giddy weeks talking on the phone all hours of the day and night, and then their first days back in the same city with one another.

London.

Where they didn't leave her suite at The Ritz. Where they consummated their passion and cemented their devotion to one another. Before reality intruded and everything went wrong.

'What are you doing here?' she asked.

'What am I...? What are you doing here? Were you looking for me?'

Her cheeks burnt. *You dumped me three days before our wedding. Why on earth would I come looking for you?* 'No, of course not. I had no idea you'd be here.'

'Oh.'

He had a point though. This was his stomping ground, his favourite pub and club. A fact that she had known when she'd suggested to Francesca that she knew somewhere fun and normal. But then *he* wasn't meant to be here. He was meant to be five thousand kilometres away on the other side of the Atlantic. Isabella suddenly had an inkling of how Elizabeth Bennet must have felt being caught visiting Pemberley.

'I thought you lived in New York.'

'I do. I'm here for a wedding. Will and Lucy's.' Rowan tipped his red head in the direction of one of the men he was with. She recognised his brother, Will. Rowan was nearly as close to Will as she was to Francesca. Will nodded and smiled, but after acknowledging her, Will looked back at Rowan and raised an eyebrow.

Heaven knew what Rowan's friends thought of her. Or his family. The press had labelled him the bad guy, but it hadn't been like that at all and Rowan's loved ones would know this. They would know the real reason why the royal wedding was cancelled with not even enough time for the caterer to cancel their order of scampi.

'It's next weekend. I flew in this morning. We're having a catch-up.'

'Like a stag night?'

'We're not calling it that.'

'Of course not.' If Isabella's cheeks had been hot before they were as obvious as a flare now.

Rowan's own stag night had marked the beginning of the end. That incident, on top of the stories about his family, his father in particular, had been the final straw. Rowan had come to her to let her know that he couldn't do it. He couldn't, as much as he might want to, marry a princess and put himself, his friends or his family under that sort of scrutiny. It wasn't fair and it wasn't right.

She'd had to keep her emotions in check and play it cool to avoid even further drama so she'd told him she understood, that she didn't blame him. They had both thought he'd be able to handle it, but neither of them had counted on the fact the media would go after his family. They had rushed too quickly into their engagement. And she'd wondered, deep down and in the early hours of the morning, if it had all been her fault anyway. She'd been so infatuated she'd pushed him into it before he'd been ready.

'I assumed you were in the States and I had such a good time when you brought me here. I wanted to bring Francesca out for the night. Have some fun. Pretend…' *Pretend everything is normal, pretend my father isn't sick, pretend you still love me.* She didn't have to finish her sentence but he nodded. He knew. He'd always understood her.

'I'm sorry to hear your father's unwell. How's he doing?'

The kindness in his voice rippled through her body and nearly broke her. She felt tears rising behind her eyes and sniffed. Rowan reached up and pressed his open palm to her bare elbow. Simultaneously comforting and supporting her. Her legs swayed and her body wanted to fall into him and let him catch her in every imaginable way. But she locked her knees firmly in place and swallowed the tears back.

'He's not out of the woods yet.'

Out of the corner of her eye she saw a few of the other patrons were looking surreptitiously in their direction. Standing alone, she wouldn't attract much attention, but with Francesca people always recognised her. Now—standing with Rowan—she was equally identifiable.

'People are looking,' she whispered. He should leave. She should leave. This whole thing must end. She searched the bar hopelessly for Francesca. 'I should go.'

'No, not like this. You're upset. Come with me.'

'Where?'

With his hand on her elbow, his fingertips burning a brand on her skin and sending her pulse skyrocketing, he steered her into an alcove just off the bar.

'What the…?' was all she could say before he'd opened the closest door and looked inside. It was small and dark except for some ambient light coming in via a small high window. He nudged her inside. She expected him to leave but he stepped in as well and closed the door with an ominous click.

Out of the frying pan, so to speak.

'Are we allowed in here?'

'Your Highness, I'm sure no one will mind.' He smiled at her properly for the first time that evening. It was the same smile that used to make her insides somersault but now it made her blood cool.

'Please don't call me that.'

'Why not?'

'Because it's not my name.'

'Under the circumstances...'

'Under the circumstances I think you should call me by my name. We're not strangers and calling me by my title won't change that.'

Rowan lowered his head and he spoke to the floor. 'Your Highness... I'm doing it for me, as much as you.'

She shouldn't have come here. Should have chosen somewhere else. Or not sneaked out of the coronation party to begin with. Stayed and looked for one of the men on her mother's 'approved' list.

Prior to their engagement, her father's office had coordinated and released information about Rowan, his childhood and business successes. Her parents had adored Rowan, Francesca had too. Mostly because they could see how much Rowan and Isabella loved one another. It was more than simple attraction—though that was undeniable—they clicked. They shared views and values and a sense of humour. If her family had any reservations about their relationship they had kept them to themselves.

Isabella had not seen any issues; she didn't

think she could've imagined a better life partner. Rowan was everything she was looking for: kind and intelligent. Interesting and interested. And he made her laugh.

They planned to divide their time between Monterossa and London. He would continue his work; she would continue to represent the royal family. They believed they could make it work. They became engaged six months after meeting, and set to wed six months after that. In hindsight it was too quick, but no one was going to tell the Isabella and Rowan of eighteen months ago that.

She should have paid more attention to the cracks that began to appear when their engagement was announced. More attention to what was being said about Rowan beyond the official messages being circulated by the palace.

Isabella didn't pay much attention to social media. She never had. It was one of the strategies she used to manage her mental health. She trusted the palace staff to tell her what she wanted to know and didn't let the background noise of the twenty-four-hour news cycle intrude into her thoughts.

Rowan did notice though. He knew what was being said about his family. How reporters were trying to contact his friends, waiting outside their homes, their workplaces. How they were even so desperate as to contact schoolteachers he hadn't spoken to in a decade and a half.

She advised him to ignore it, not to go on social media. As if that would make the problem go away. He tried to, for a while, but he couldn't ignore the reports from his friends and family about what was happening to them.

It all came to a head in the weeks before the wedding as press scrutiny intensified. The stories about his father, his mother. His brother. Rowan's childhood. With a family who had been innocently minding their own business until their son became engaged to a princess. They didn't deserve the headlines.

'We pay for the royal family! We have a right to know!' screamed the pundits.

And maybe they were right.

But no one paid Rowan, or his family and friends, and the world did not have a right to their business. Or their lives.

It had been a calm break-up. No screaming, no fighting. Just soft tears of resignation. He'd taken her for a walk in the palace grounds—not to her favourite place, along the walls near the sea, as though he'd known that the conversation they were going to have would ruin that place for her for ever, but to a secluded garden she didn't often visit. And he'd sat her down on a bench under a magnolia tree and told her that he was sorry but that he couldn't do it. He couldn't do it to his family and friends. That even though he cared for her, it wasn't going to work.

He'd helped her family undo all the arrangements, offered to pay whatever needed to be paid, an offer that had been refused by her parents, and then he'd left. Left her to cry the hard, angry tears alone. In private.

So when he said calling her 'Your Highness' was self-preservation, she reluctantly understood.

They could never go back to how things were.

'What would you like me to call you?'

Rowan stepped back, but the room they were in was really just a large cupboard, and he bumped into the door.

'What do you mean?'

'Would you like me to call you Mr James?'

'Are you joking?'

'No. But I can tell you want to maintain distance between us.'

'Yes, but…you are a princess, Your Highness.'

'I'm not different from you.'

He sighed long and deep. 'Rowan, call me Rowan, Isabella.'

As soon as he said her name she realised her mistake. The syllables rippled through her, like a wave. Pleasure laced with the sharpest of pains.

She stepped back, instantly bumping something hard with the small of her back. Now her eyes had adjusted to the dim light she saw that they were indeed in some sort of cupboard. The boxes were labelled with liquor names, spirits and wines.

She laughed. 'Want a drink?'

'Heck, yes,' he said and they both laughed.

'I'm sorry I came here,' she said.

'Don't be. I know you liked it. I always wanted to bring you back.'

'And here we are.'

'Did you say Francesca is here as well?'

'Yes, out there somewhere. We were at the Duke of Oxford's party.'

'And you left that to come here?'

'Yes.'

A crease appeared between his eyes.

'Things have been hard at home. I wanted a little break. I wanted Francesca to have a break.'

The crease deepened. 'Isn't that risky?'

'It's just for a few hours. A chance to escape…'

'I'm so sorry things have been hard for you. And I'm sorry about your father.'

At the mention of her father, of everything that had passed between her and Rowan, she swallowed back the lump.

This was silly! She'd been strong, she was okay! Being back with Rowan for a few moments, suddenly the defences she'd built around herself began to crumble. She shook herself. She just needed to get out of here, find Francesca and a Rowan-free bar instead.

'I'm sorry I haven't been able to be there for you, through all this.'

She had to get out quickly!

'I do understand, you know. I don't blame you.'
More lies. But what choice did she have? There
was already enough drama in her family. She had
to stay calm.

Rowan's Adam's apple bobbed with a deep
swallow. 'Thank you. The last thing I wanted to
do was hurt you.'

But he had hurt her. And being in this cupboard
with her, he continued to do so.

'It just wasn't meant to be.'

'I'm sorry I wasn't strong enough,' he added.

'What? No. Don't say that.'

She'd thought it. Wished he had been able to
set aside his reservations for her, but every time
she had thought that she'd realised that that would
have made him care less about his family and
friends and *that* would have made her love him
less. It was easier to lie, to tell the world she understood. That she was fine.

'I'm sorry as well.'

'What for?'

'Not giving it all up.'

'What on earth are you talking about?'

It was one of the many possibilities she'd
thought through in the horrible days after the
wedding that wasn't. Leaving Monterossa and
running away with him, somewhere different.
Somewhere anonymous. The end of the world.

'I had this thought that we could run away to
New Zealand.'

'New Zealand?'

'It's the most remote place I could think of. It's meant to be pretty. They have good wine, rugby… it sounds great.'

He shook his head. 'I think they still have newspapers and photographers in New Zealand.'

'I think they do too, and I don't think being a princess is something you can ever actually give up. If anything, people become more interested in you if you try to walk away.'

'Yes, I think you're right. But, Isabella…' Rowan leant forward and it didn't take much before he was close enough to her that she could feel the warmth from his tall, strong body surrounding hers, seeping into every one of her pores. 'I would never have asked you to do that.'

In the dim light of the room she could only just make out the angle of his jaw and the hard lines of his shoulders. She could feel him though. They weren't touching, but every cell in her body knew he was close and thrummed and vibrated accordingly. Stupid cells, stupid body.

'I know. I wanted to let you know…that I thought of it. I thought of everything.'

'I thought of everything as well. I thought of every way we could possibly make it work. Believe me. I did.'

She nodded and looked down because if she looked into his amber eyes the emotion she'd been pushing down would probably flood over.

He slid two fingers into her hair and twirled them around a lock, but he might as well have taken her heart into his hands by the way in which her insides twisted. She closed her eyes and breathed him in again for the last time. If she didn't pull herself away now she didn't think she'd be able to.

'I'll get Francesca and we'll leave. I should've thought this through better. I'm sorry for coming.'

'Don't be. It was nice to see you.'

'Really?' Isabella laughed, at the same time as she was still biting back tears.

'You'll always be special to me.'

Special. That was all she was. Like a friend. Not a soul mate. Not a one and only.

It was goodbye. A bow tied around the goodbye they had shared last year. But this time it was final. This time they both understood why it had to be and had made their peace with it.

'We should go,' she said, the weight of everything pressing against her chest, the air in the room suddenly non-existent.

CHAPTER THREE

TAKING ISABELLA OUT of the way of prying eyes had seemed like a good plan, until he'd unintentionally directed her into a cupboard the size of a toilet cubicle.

It was difficult enough dismissing thoughts of Isabella when she was a continent away. He'd barely managed to control his heart rate when she was standing across the bar from him, but now, with her perfume swirling around his head like a dense fog, he felt control slipping from his grasp.

It had just taken every ounce of his self-control not to pull Isabella to him and tell her he'd made a horrible mistake. Thankfully, she saved him from himself when she said they should go. Isabella would leave as soon as she located her sister and this would truly be the last time he saw her.

They emerged from the cupboard, blinking in the comparative brightness. A man stood between them and the rest of the room. He was holding up a camera. The man wasn't just using his phone, but had a camera, with a professional-looking flash, and he was pointing it in their direction.

Rowan groaned. Hadn't he learnt anything? Of course some grubby pap would be waiting for them to come out of the small room together.

'Princess! Rowan! Are you back together?' yelled the photographer. A flash illuminated Isabella's perfect face and she squeaked with fright. Rowan turned his back to the camera, wrapping his arm around Isabella to shield her as the flashes flickered around them both, the camera capturing everything.

Was there nothing these bastards wouldn't do?

'We have to get out of here. Is there a back door?' she asked.

Something in Rowan snapped. This was his bar, *his* place. Everyone in here had a right to privacy. He wasn't going to go through this again. He wasn't going to wake up tomorrow morning to a headline that they were back together when that would be nothing more than a heartbreaking lie.

He drew a deep breath and turned to the man. 'Give me your camera.'

The photographer laughed, but not before he took one last photo of Rowan staring him down, with Isabella next to him, her hand on his arm. Her cheeks still flushed from their encounter.

No. They were not going to get this photo. This headline. This *lie*.

'You heard him—give us the camera,' Isabella said.

A crowd had gathered behind the photographer, mostly interested strangers, but Rowan noticed Will and their friend Rob, an ex-rugby player. They stepped up, blocking the man's path.

The photographer turned his body and tried to weave his way through the crowd. Isabella yelled, 'Stop him!' across the bar.

Will and the others moved to encircle the man but with a quick turn he slipped past. With blood rushing in his head and Isabella's words echoing in his ears, Rowan moved after the man, chasing him to the stairwell. The other patrons slowed the photographer's path long enough for Rowan to catch him and grab his sleeve.

'Stop. Give us your damn camera. At least delete the photos.'

The man looked down at Rowan's hand on his own arm then glared at Rowan with a challenge. *Are you seriously going to make this physical?*

Knowing that would instantly take the situation from salvageable to sensational, Rowan let go of the man's arm. The photographer bolted. A chuckle floated behind him as he bounded down the last steps and out of the front door. 'Give it up, mate,' he yelled.

But Rowan would not give it up.

And he was not his *mate*.

They were not getting one more falsehood about him out into the world. Rowan bounded down the steps two at a time and followed the man out into the night.

The photographer set off on foot down a nearby street. He was moving at a brisk pace but Rowan smiled to himself. His Vespa was parked just around the corner and he ran to it now. The man would not get away.

Rowan mounted his bike but as he was about to accelerate fingers curled around his arm.

'Wait for me,' Isabella pleaded.

'No, stay here. With Francesca.'

'I can't find her,' she said as she hooked a leg over the seat and climbed up behind him. 'Go!' she said.

Realising with a sigh it would be far quicker to take her with him than argue with anyone as determined as Princess Isabella, he accelerated. Rowan instantly felt her grip around him tighten as she held on, but he tried to ignore the way her palms were currently pressed against his stomach, thinking instead of the fact that neither of them were wearing helmets, and another, even more worrying headline popped into his head.

Rounding the corner, he spotted the man further down the street. While the footpaths were busy with pedestrians, the roads were reasonably clear. They followed him around a few corners, with each turn away from the Thames and the crowds. When the man stepped into the stairwell leading to a pedestrian underpass Rowan braked.

'No,' Isabella groaned.

He knew where the underpass headed. 'Get off,' he ordered.

'No, we can still catch him.'

'I know, just get off.'

Eyes wide, but thankfully not arguing, she climbed off. He opened the storage hold and took out the helmet, handing it to her. 'You'll need this.'

The smile that broadened across her face made his heart swell. But he ignored that sensation, just as he ignored the way his heart hitched as she ran her hand up his arm and climbed back on the bike.

'Hold on,' he said, this time bracing himself for the sensation of Isabella's soft curves pressing against his back. It helped. A little.

The underpass had two exits and he had to choose which was more likely. The one that led back to the Thames and the City or the other.

He chose the second. As they rounded the corner and the exit came into view he smiled—the man was walking quickly along the end of the road. Rowan accelerated. Isabella held on even tighter and his limbs tingled with the sparks zipping up and down them even faster than the bike was travelling.

They caught up to the man just as he stopped

outside an apartment building. Rowan pulled up and cut the engine as Isabella slid off the bike. She ran, with helmet still on, to the door but reached it just as it clicked shut. Rowan stayed behind, realising the futility of her mission. She pushed and tugged on the door handle and of course it didn't give.

The building was modern, sleek and had about a dozen door buzzers. Few enough that they could try them all, though Rowan knew this man would be the one who didn't answer. Isabella pulled the helmet off and ran her hands through her soft, shiny hair, fluffing it out and up. The vision did nothing to calm his already elevated heart rate.

They stood in the streetlight, facing one another. She had her hands on her hips, he put his face in his.

'It was worth a try,' he said.

'Of course it was worth a try.'

'Come on, I'll take you back to Francesca.'

'It's still worth trying. You're not giving up this easily, are you?'

Giving up. Easily.

The words tore at his deepest fears. His deepest regrets.

He was a school dropout. A princess dumper. That was his thing—he gave up.

'You want us to press each buzzer? He won't answer.'

'No, but if we can just get into the building.'

As though her words had summoned it, a couple emerged from the elevator and headed in their direction.

Without speaking, Rowan turned to the Vespa and secured it. Isabella walked to the door as the couple were departing, catching the handle just before the door shut. The couple didn't look back and Isabella and Rowan slipped into the building as though they were meant to be there. She marched up to the lift and pressed the call button. It opened immediately and they stepped inside, but Rowan instantly saw the problem.

As he expected, the elevator required a code before it would take them to the upper levels.

She stomped a red stiletto-clad foot and he grinned.

'Damn. I thought we had him,' she said.

'He's not just going to hand the photo over.'

'But if we offer him money, more than he can sell it for?'

'He's probably posted it already.'

Rowan looked around the building they were in; it was a reasonably upmarket place. This man wasn't just an opportunist, most likely he did this for a living. Rowan couldn't even begin to guess what he'd been doing in Twilight. For all Rowan knew, he'd followed the Princesses from the party. If the man was trying to find a buyer for the photo they might have more time, though not much. It was only that thought and the glimmer of hope it provided that stopped him saying, 'Let's go.'

Instead he sighed.

Isabella shook her head, backed against the wall and sank to the floor. Rowan copied her action.

'We can't stay here all night,' she said.

'I don't want him to sell or post that photo any more than you do.'

He knew why he didn't want this photo to get out. He'd spent the last year trying to get the world to forget him. This would enliven all the attention on him and his family once again.

But Isabella? Scrutiny was part of her life. What was one more photo?

She's ashamed of you. You always knew you were never good enough for a beautiful princess. You might be rich now, but everyone knows where you came from. Everyone knows you're a dropout. A failure.

'It won't be the first time we've been photographed together.' He tried to keep the hurt out of his tone and wasn't sure if he'd succeeded.

'Of course not, but I do know this is the exact sort of thing you've been trying to avoid.'

That stumped him for a moment. 'Exactly. It's my problem. You should go.'

Isabella turned to him, placed her hand on his. 'It's my problem as well. We may not be together but I hope we're still friends.'

His throat tightened. Friends was an optimistic hope. He couldn't imagine a time when he was 'just friends' with Isabella. That would imply that a part of him no longer longed for something more. From where he sat now, that seemed as far away as it had one year ago.

He gently slid his arm out from under her hand.

'We are friends, and I'm sorry I got you into this situation. You should go. I'll stay and do what I can.'

'What on earth are you talking about?'

'I'm sorry you were photographed with me. I should've been more careful.'

'You keep saying "I". We used to be "we",' she said softly.

Yes, but that was before...

'And you sound like you think I'm ashamed of being caught with you,' she added.

'Aren't you?'

I dumped you and now I've got you into this mess.

She looked into her lap. 'I've never been ashamed. Not of what happened. And certainly never of you.' She looked him straight in the eye and it was as though she'd pressed a knife against his gut. He was bound to the spot.

'My worries about the photo don't have anything to do with you being in it.'

'They don't?'

'Is that what you think?'

He didn't say anything, just sat there. Of course she was ashamed of being with him. He would be! Once again he'd shown how naive he could be about royalty and their relationship with the press, once again he'd let himself be photographed in an apparently compromising position.

'I wasn't meant to be at Twilight. I'm meant to be at the Ashton, in Mayfair, with two thousand other people, representing my country at a party being hosted by the Duke of Oxford. I don't want it getting out that I left the party. I don't want my parents knowing I let them down and encouraged Francesca to do the same.'

It wasn't about him. She didn't hate him. It was something worse, something important. It wasn't simply embarrassment. It was a fear of upsetting her already worried parents.

'I'm not embarrassed about being seen with *you*. I'm worried about embarrassing my parents. And my sister.'

She crossed her arms and lowered her head. Conversation over.

Rowan stood, wandered around the foyer. Counted the number of door buzzers, stared at the generic print on the wall. Wondered how he'd ended up here.

Two years ago his life had been on its upward trajectory. Busy, but relatively uncomplicated. The relationships he'd had in the past had been pleasant and satisfying, but they hadn't upended his life.

And then he'd walked in a hotel bar in Geneva and everything had changed. While he didn't regret breaking off his engagement with Isabella, if he had to go back to a moment in time, it would be to that night. Where it all began. To when life was straightforward and he hadn't been forced to choose between the two things he loved the most. It had been an excruciating decision to make, but he'd known that it would be easier in the end for Isabella. She would find someone else who could handle the attention and he would have his business and his family. It had been painful, but it had all worked out.

Isabella was better off without him, and it showed. Seeing her here tonight, so strong, so confident, so completely over him, he knew he'd made the right decision. He'd always felt more for her than she did for him. His heart had been a wild beating mess, hers had continued to beat calmly and serenely.

'Is that why you really left?'

Her voice was soft and he wasn't sure he'd heard her or imagined her. He turned back to her. She was looking up at him, eyes wide and her gorgeous face open and vulnerable. His heart cracked.

'What do you mean?'

'Did you leave because you thought you weren't good enough?'

He scoffed.

'Of course not. I mean, there's no denying we're from very different backgrounds.'

'In some ways. But not in all ways. We both care about things. We both work hard, we both want to make a difference. That sounds pretty similar to me.'

Those were the same things he'd told himself for the first year: that their backgrounds didn't matter because they had their future in common. But it wasn't true. He'd been so ridiculously optimistic. Dazzled by his feelings for Isabella.

'I didn't leave because I didn't think I was good enough. I left because I hadn't realised how much pressure there would be on me, my family and my friends. I shouldn't have been so naive. I will always be sorry for that.'

She nodded and Rowan sat back down next to her. He wasn't sure why. He knew they should leave, get back to Twilight or go home.

'You could let your parents know first? About the photo.'

'No. At least, not tonight. Not yet.'

'Then shouldn't you let Francesca know where you are?'

'No to that as well. She'll be fine. She looked like she was having a good time. She probably hasn't realised I've left yet. I want to sort this out before I go back.'

Isabella took out her phone, switched it off and slipped it back into her small bag.

He raised an eyebrow in question.

'I don't want her calling me.'

'Can't she track you?' He remembered that both sisters' and their parents' phones had the geolocators switched on so they could see where the others were.

'We switched that off before we came out. Didn't want Mum and Dad knowing.'

He tried not to let the shock on his face show.

She really had broken palace protocol this evening. She'd be in a lot of trouble if they found out what she'd done.

'It's not like they can ground us, I mean, we're grown women but...'

He nodded. You never stopped being your parents' children. You still worried about your parents and they worried about you. He understood completely. That was why he was waiting here on this pointless mission as well: so as not to upset his family further.

'How has she been? Francesca?' he asked.

'Good, but it's been a difficult past few months for both of us.'

While news about the Monterossan royal family was rarely something he sought out, he had occasionally looked for updates about the King's health. Leonardo was a good man, and always welcoming and generous to Rowan. He had also been understanding when Rowan had called off the engagement.

'Better to do it now than after the wedding. I appreciate this would have taken a great deal of bravery,' the King had said to him.

As well as being concerned about their father's health, the sisters would have been working extra hard as well. Royals didn't get time off to grieve—if anything they had to work harder in times of illness and death. No wonder Isabella and Francesca had wanted to slip away for an evening and forget all their worries and responsibilities.

'How have *you* been doing? Really?'

Isabella gave him a shy shrug. 'I'm okay. It's been hard since Dad was diagnosed, but weirdly all the extra work has been distracting. And that's been good. Is that silly?'

'Not at all. I often find distraction and solace in work. Sometimes it's the one thing that's easiest to control.'

He'd never spoken truer words; his job, his business, had been his one solace in the past year.

'How's New York?' she asked.

He told her how he'd come to love the pace, the people. How he felt he'd settled in and how good it had been for him professionally. He didn't mention his personal life, not that there was anything to say about that. Since Isabella, he'd steered well clear of any entanglements, casual or otherwise.

The conversation meandered easily into all sorts of other topics: movies, music, books. They had so much catching up to do. He remembered all the many things he'd wanted to tell her over the past year and she did as well. Little, big, funny, sad. He didn't know how much time had passed and was barely aware of the elevator bell dinging, signalling someone entering the foyer.

It was him.

The photographer. The man froze at first, wide eyed and shocked. Rowan and Isabella scrambled up, just as the photographer was putting two and two together. He looked back, as if to go back to the elevator, but Isabella, who was closest, blocked his path. Rowan then stepped to the front door. Goodness knew what they both thought they would do to stop the man if he really wanted to run, but he didn't. He stood in the middle of the foyer and laughed.

'You cannot be serious. You chased me here?'

'Please don't publish the photograph. It was nothing, really, we aren't back together,' Isabella blurted.

The man looked from Isabella to Rowan and back again and smirked. Rowan's chest burnt. He didn't appreciate the man's judgement.

'Seriously, publishing the photos will just cause

further hurt to our families. How much do you want? We will beat it,' Rowan said.

The man narrowed his eyes, continued to look between the pair. Laughed again.

'Royals hunting down paparazzi? That's a new one.' He laughed again. Rowan was beginning to get very sick of the sound of the man's cackle.

'Tell us what you want; we'll pay it,' Isabella said.

'It's too late.'

'You posted it?' she asked.

Rowan's heart fell.

'Sold it. If I knew you were both so keen, we could've had an auction. They're great photos.'

'There's more than one?' she asked.

'Of course. There's a couple of you both before you disappeared into the cupboard. Of him comforting you. They're quite sweet. But of course the ones where you come out of the cupboard looking red-faced are great too. The one of him putting his arm around you. Really, they tell a whole story.'

He wanted to strangle this man. No. He wanted him ruined.

'Nothing happened!' she cried and the man laughed.

'Sure, sure.'

'Who to? Who did you sell it to?' Rowan asked.

'Ah, now, I can't tell you that.'

'Why not?'

'Professional ethics.'

Rowan laughed and Isabella shouted, 'Ethics? You expect us to believe that a slime ball like you has ethics?'

The man looked taken aback. 'Yes, journalistic ethics.'

'You're not a journalist,' she muttered.

Rowan agreed with her but felt the conversation slipping away from them.

'I think the public deserve to know that a princess who is meant to be at an official coronation party was in fact hiding in a cupboard in a bar on the other side the city with her ex-fiancé, don't you?'

'No, because we weren't together and it's no one else's business.'

'Isn't it? Isn't it your job, your responsibility, to be at the official function? Isn't your country paying for you to be here to represent them?'

Isabella's shoulders sagged.

Rowan clenched his fists. 'Her father is sick. Have some compassion.'

'I know her father is sick. All the more reason for her not to be gallivanting around the city—'

'You…' Rowan felt the blood rise up in him and everything went white. He stepped towards the man, unsure what on earth he was going to do. He knew what he wanted to do, but that was out of the question. He felt a warm hand on his arm.

'What my friend is trying to say is that it's been a tough few months for me, a tough year for both of us. Publishing that photo won't help. It'd be kicking two people who are already down. Please, please just tell us who you sold it to.'

'It would be against the terms of the contract. It wouldn't be honourable.'

Honour? Rowan bit back the words. He knew this man was scum. He was just protecting his money, nothing else.

'Can you give us a hint, then?' Isabella asked.

'What do you mean?'

They looked helplessly to one another then back to the man.

'Twenty questions. You just say yes or no. You won't say the name. It'll be fun.'

'If that's your idea of fun, you need to get out more. No, wait, that's what got us here in the first place.'

'Did you sell it to a newspaper publisher?' asked Isabella.

He was slow to answer but eventually said, 'Yes.'

'London based?' asked Rowan.

The man nodded.

'Broadsheet?' Rowan asked, hoping the answer would be yes, rather than the other choice, tabloid.

The man shook his head.

'Does it start with T?' Isabella asked.

The man nodded and grinned.

'They all start with T, because they all start with *The*…' Rowan whispered to her.

'Oh, yes. Does the second word start with T?' Isabella asked.

The man nodded again and said, 'You're right, this has been fun. But if you'll excuse me…' He slipped past them both, out of the door and into the night.

The Truth?' she guessed. It was an ironically named paper, known for printing anything but.

'It has to be.'

'Well, that's the end of it. The photos will be all over the place tomorrow. We should go,' said Rowan.

'No.' Isabella shook her head and looked out of the door. 'We're going to talk to them. Ask them not to print it.'

'The paper? The editor?'

'No. The owner.'

'How? Do you know him?'

'Never met him.'

'Then how?' Rowan had always admired her energy and optimism, but now feared her positivity was bordering on delusion.

'Because I know where he's going to be tonight and, what's more, I have an invitation.' There was a glimmer in her eyes that made his heart lift.

'The party at the Ashton?'

'Yes.'

'Who is he?'

'Sir Liam Goldsworthy. He owns a publishing company, magazines, books, but also *The Truth*.'

'Why did he get an invite to the party if he publishes a tabloid like *The Truth*?'

'Ah, because of his wife. She's been friends with the new Queen for ever. Besides, with the usual hypocrisy tabloids are famous for, *The Truth* likes to focus on Hollywood celebs and European royalty. Tends to leave the Brits alone.'

'Got it. But you've never met him?'

'Never!' she said, as though this were a good thing.

Rowan glanced at his watch. It was close to ten p.m. He thought her chances were next to zero, but said, 'I guess it's worth a shot.'

'Absolutely it is. Come on.'

'You want me to come?'

'You've got the bike. I don't fancy my chances of hailing a cab on a night like tonight.'

'Do you want me to drive you there?'

'Yes, absolutely. We're in this together.'

'And I'll just wait outside the front door for you?'

'Don't be silly. We'll sneak in the back. The same way I sneaked out.'

'You said you had an invitation.'

'I do, but I can hardly just walk in the front door.'

It was late and Rowan was still on New York time but according to his body clock he'd just missed a night's sleep.

'I'm not following.'

'And you're meant to be the smart one.'

His cheeks warmed at the compliment.

'I don't want to make an entrance. Besides, the party started hours ago. How would it look if I arrive three hours late, especially when everyone thought I was already there? No, you have to help me sneak in the back. Once I'm in, no one can say anything because I'm meant to be there so they can't kick me out.'

He shook his head. It seemed unnecessary, but he was prepared to drive her to the Ashton. Even if it meant more time with her arms wrapped around his waist, her soft chest pressing against his back, and her thighs tightly gripping his.

Steel. You are made of steel.

'How about this? We try the back door and if that doesn't work, we go in the front,' she said.

Her continued use of the word 'we' troubled him, but he chose to believe it was an oversight rather than intentional.

'Lead on,' he said, heart sinking.

CHAPTER FOUR

IT WASN'T EXACTLY *Roman Holiday.*

Audrey Hepburn had looked so free and delighted on the back of that Vespa, whereas Isabella gripped Rowan as if her life depended on it, and indeed it did. She could barely open her eyes, let alone enjoy the wind in her hair. Much of the traffic—endless lanes of cabs—was largely at a standstill. But a Vespa? A Vespa could weave in and out of the slow-moving traffic at a great pace. And Rowan did. They had made their way over London Bridge and were now hurtling along the embankment towards the West End.

Rowan was right: for all her bravado she thought there was a very slim chance she'd be let back into the hotel via the back door. And even if she was, then what? How would she find Sir Liam? What if he'd left the party already? What would she say to him? What if he said no?

Even though these were the problems she should have been solving as they ducked in and out of traffic, all she could think about was how thin Rowan's cotton shirt was. How she could feel the warmth of his back against her chest. How she didn't want to hold his torso too tight because when she did she could feel his stomach, his washboard abs. How snuggly her thighs were wrapped around his. How the whole thing was making desire fizz up inside her, through her legs, and into her core.

When he was an ocean away her longing for him was painful, but theoretical. Now she was wrapped around him. Literally. And she wanted to explode.

Keeping her desire in check was one thing. She could probably manage that.

But keeping in her emotions? Holding her shattered heart together? This wasn't just a man she was attracted to. This was *Rowan*. The love of her life. Her tragically star-crossed love. The man she could never be with.

The man who didn't love her enough to be with her.

She understood the practicalities. The reasons. After all, she understood the pressure of being in the public eye. She felt its weight with every step she took.

Hold your head up. Smile. Be polite. Don't offend.

She knew that her behaviour reflected not just on her, but on her family. On Monterossa. She'd been told, before she could even talk herself, that she had to watch what she did and said in front of anyone. More than that, she knew what it was like to have your slightest failings magnified and analysed, to have lies spoken about you.

And she wouldn't wish the scrutiny she had endured on anyone she cared for.

Yet...

A small part of her—the smallest part, the part that woke her at two a.m.—asked, 'Why didn't he love me enough?'

When the sun came up each morning, reason returned. She wasn't enough because no one would be. No one sensible would want to marry her and have their life dragged through the muckraking of the press. And she didn't want to be with someone who wasn't sensible.

But that was a problem for later. She had to figure out what to do *now*. They zipped along Piccadilly and Regent Street, Union Jacks and red, white and blue bunting hung across the road, the streets still swelled with people. They were only a few blocks from the Ashton.

Then what?

You don't need to know how to fix it. You just need to do the next right thing.

But she had no idea what the next right thing was.

This had all been her stupid idea—*Go out on the town! Leave your security! Live like a normal person!*—and now here she was, on the back of a Vespa, hurtling through London on the way to sneak back into the party she'd just sneaked out of.

But with her ex.

There had been bad photos of her taken before. The time she'd had too many cosmopolitans on her eighteenth birthday and brought most of them back up into a nearby fountain. The time she'd accidentally tucked her skirt into her pants during a break in the middle of her father's birthday concert. But this, while she was fully clothed and sober, was bad. Her parents and her country would know she had neglected her duties and convinced her sister to as well.

And with her father's health so precarious. Nausea rose in her stomach. And it was not the fact that she was wearing the single helmet, or that Rowan had only narrowly missed a cab in his hurry to get them to the Ashton. No. It was the fear of her father finding out what she'd done and the look she'd see on her mother's face.

You'll figure out a way. You always do.

That voice again.

Her sister's voice.

Isabella looked around almost expecting to see her, as she had always been, every day of Isabella's life. But she wasn't there.

And soon that could become a permanent state of affairs.

Isabella pushed that thought aside as well.

They approached a set of lights that had just

turned amber and she expected Rowan to stop, but instead he accelerated and went through the junction as the lights changed to red. Isabella did what she'd been trying not to do and clutched Rowan tighter. She tried not to think about how good she felt with her chest pressed against his back, her breasts pushing against him. Her poor nipples standing to attention.

He braked suddenly and she was pushed against him again, causing more friction and pleasure. When would this ride be over?

She wasn't even a teenager when she first realised that the world expected her to be rebel. She was the second and therefore the naughty one. But Isabella had no desire to be a rebel, she didn't want to upset her family, she just wanted to do some good in the world. Only she didn't know what that looked like for her. Raising money for charity? Visiting hospitals? All worthy, but none felt right for her. Isabella had plenty of second-born princesses to look to as role models, but the one she identified with most was the fictional Princess Anna. This—a pointless chase through London on the back of a Vespa—was a very Princess Anna thing to do.

She laughed and Rowan turned his head with a confused look.

'Watch where you're going!' she yelped.

The world wanted her to be a rebel, because that was the stereotype. They looked for misbehaviour, watched for her to step out of line. And she wouldn't give them the satisfaction. She was going to track down Sir Liam and get him to stop publication of the photo.

If only she knew how.

The public were fascinated by Isabella to a degree they weren't with other second-borns. Royal twins were rare, but royal twins directly in line to the throne were practically unheard of. People always wanted to know if she was upset she'd missed out on the crown by five minutes. What no one appreciated was that everything about royal succession was arbitrary and accidental. It made little difference to be five minutes behind in the line of succession or five years.

Except that, being the same age, she and Francesca were brought up together. They did everything together. When she'd been fifteen and decided she would much rather stay at the local school she was at than go to the boarding school in Milan her parents had in mind, she'd had an argument with her father.

'I don't see why I have to do the same training as Francesca.'

'To support her.'

'But I won't ever be queen.' Isabella had always been happy about this. Relieved almost. She saw what her father did and it didn't look like fun to her.

'Besides, you'll be qualified for many jobs.

Diplomat. Queen consort,' her father had said and Isabella had bristled.

'I thought we didn't do that any longer.'

'What?'

'Trade off spare princesses in diplomatic deals.'

'You're second in line to this throne,' her father said.

'So? I may as well be fiftieth! When Francesca has kids I may as well be commoner.'

'That's not true. Supporting your sister is a very important role. Being a monarch is a lonely, lonely job. It's important to have someone with you who understands you and the job.'

'But when she marries…'

And her father didn't have an answer for that.

At the moment her sister wasn't close to marrying. Since her break-up with Benigno, Francesca's love life had been as uneventful as Isabella's had been lately. But one day Francesca would find someone who would sweep her off her feet and then where would that leave Isabella? Third wheel? No longer the spare, just someone who used to be famous. Isabella wasn't sure how she felt about that. Either way.

Francesca's accession to the throne had always seemed like a far-off event, but even though no one came right out and said anything things were changing. Isabella felt it.

Rowan drove past the front of the hotel. Outside the grand entrance were several people milling about in their party clothes. The hotel was still brightly lit, from inside and out. The party was still in full swing.

He drove around the corner and into a laneway. Once the bike stopped Isabella was even more conscious of their closeness, his warmth. The beat of her heart, which had been drowned out by the motor, was now thumping in her ears so loudly she wondered if Rowan could actually hear it. She unhooked her arms from around his torso and they began the process of disentangling themselves from one another and getting off the bike.

Rowan looked as though he was also catching his breath. His face slightly red, his hair wild from the ride. He ran his hands through it and looked around. 'Are we being ridiculous?'

'No more ridiculous than this whole situation.'

He was as unsure as she was. One of them had to be the brave one. And at this moment that looked as if it would have to be her.

'How do you propose we sneak in?'

'Relax, it's not as if it's Buckingham Palace.'

Bravado was not the same as bravery and she hoped he didn't notice the tremor in her voice.

'Won't there be heaps of security? Think of all the dignitaries who are here.'

She waved his question away. 'The US president isn't here. It's mostly minor royals, aristocracy. For instance, like the Earl of Hereford. The

Count of Westphalia,' she said, remembering her mother's list.

'That seems like a very precise list.'

Her cheeks flushed. She led the way around to the exit she, Francesca and their bodyguard, Giovanni Gallo, had come out of several hours earlier. Isabella had always just thought that security was there to protect her. It was never something she had to figure out a way around.

Except tonight.

'Should I distract them? Point to the sky and yell, "Look!" so you can sneak in?' he asked.

'Please tell me you're not serious?'

'At this point I don't know what I am.'

She shook her head. Nor did she.

'No, here's what we'll do. I'll just tell them who I am. We need to get you in as well.'

'Me? I can't come.'

'Why not?'

'I'm not invited. It'll attract more attention. You don't need me.'

He would've kept reeling off excuses if she hadn't reached over and placed her hand on his forearm. 'I do need you. I don't know what I'm going to say.'

Rowan shook his head. 'I don't know either.'

'Between us we can come up with something. Please, can we just try?'

When he'd come to her, three days before the wedding, and told her they needed to talk, she hadn't begged. He'd set out his case so clearly and rationally.

'The press intrusion is more than I thought it would be. My parents and friends are being placed under unreasonable pressure. I can't marry you.'

She hadn't argued or begged. She'd wanted him to marry her willingly and happily. Not under pressure. She hadn't even cried. Not until much, much later.

But now she needed him. Just this one thing. And then they would say goodbye for ever and she'd never set foot in a country again without first ascertaining his whereabouts.

'I won't ask you anything else. Ever. Please. Come in with me.'

He looked at the dark sky and she squeezed his forearm. It was just as strong and firm as it had always been. Her insides melted. She wanted to press her face against his chest and sob.

'I'm not going to sneak and I'm not going to fight,' he said.

She smiled and pulled him by the hand. 'Of course not.'

They approached the two security guards standing outside a nondescript door. Isabella knew it was the back entrance to the Ashton, because she and Francesca had let themselves out of it several hours earlier. She made a mental note to remember to reassure Francesca that she was okay in a way that didn't prompt questions. She wanted to have this whole thing fixed before she dragged the heir to the throne into it.

Isabella recognised the guards, a tall woman and a shorter man. A man carrying two large rubbish bags exited the door and the security guards stepped out of his way.

'Come on,' Isabella whispered and grabbed Rowan's hand. His hand in hers was no less tempting than her thighs wrapped around his, but it did make her feel better. Besides, she didn't want to risk him chickening out and doing a runner.

The guards straightened their backs as Isabella and Rowan approached. 'Hello! You remember us, don't you?' Isabella said.

The guards exchanged a look.

'I'm Princess Isabella of Monterossa and this is Rowan James, my plus one. We were at the party earlier and now we need to go back in.'

'This isn't a concert. You can't come and go.'

'Of course not, but since you saw us both leave earlier, and since I don't want to have to embarrass anyone by going back in the front entrance, I thought you could help us be discreet by letting us back in.'

The woman shook her head. 'We don't do that.'

As she finished speaking, the man with the rubbish bags returned empty-handed and the man opened the door for him.

'He didn't have an invitation,' Rowan said.

'He works here,' said the woman.

'And we're guests. You saw us. Me and my sister.' Isabella directed that remark to the man who had definitely seen her, Francesca and Gallo. He'd even said, 'Have fun, ladies,' as they'd left.

The man studied Rowan. 'Is he the man you left with?'

'Of course he is. Don't you remember? You're a security guard!'

Her heart was thumping in her throat as she waited to see if her bluff worked. She hoped that in the darkness he wouldn't have noticed the fact that their bodyguard, Giovanni Gallo, had classic Mediterranean looks while Rowan's red-headed ancestors hailed from Scotland.

The woman rolled her eyes and turned away. The man then reached behind and opened the door to them.

A rush of relief and adrenaline ran through her. They were in!

The hotel looked different from this angle. She hadn't paid much attention to the layout as they were leaving. To her right she could hear the unmistakable sounds of a large kitchen and her stomach rumbled. When had she eaten last? As soon as she'd spoken to Sir Liam they would definitely find something.

'This way,' she said, and directed Rowan away from the kitchens. They walked along a quiet corridor and then up half a flight of stairs she recognised from when she'd walked down them earlier.

At the top of the stairs they could hear the music and laughter coming from the main ballroom and it was clear where the party was.

'Wait,' he said and pulled her to one side, just as she heard people approaching from around the corner. Rowan opened the nearest door and tugged her inside. The room was dark and they both fumbled around for a light switch, Rowan eventually locating and tugging on a string that turned on a flickering yellowish light above them.

It was a small room, lined with boxes on one side and shelves on the other. It was bigger than the cupboard they were in at the Twilight Bar, but not by much.

'Our tour of the storerooms of London continues,' he muttered. 'I sure do know how to show a princess a good time.'

'Nonsense, these are the places you can't see on the cheap tour.'

He smiled, but his heart wasn't in it.

'I don't know what I'm doing here,' he confessed.

'Moral support.'

'Immoral, more like it.'

Then she laughed. This was why she'd wanted him by her side—because life was just better when he was.

She shoved that unhelpful thought to one side.

'We may as well put out our own press release saying we were caught in a cupboard in Twilight. I think being caught at this party could just make things worse.'

'Yes. We don't want to get caught in two confined spaces in the one night. We have to do something.'

'But what?'

You don't need to know how it ends...you just need to do the next thing.

Isabella looked around where they were now. A different sort of storeroom. Bigger. It was lined with shelves of clothing. Uniforms to be precise.

'Ah, Rowan.'

'I'm not going to like what you're about to suggest, am I?'

'That depends on whether you brought your adventurous spirt.'

She pulled out a cropped black jacket from a nearby shelf and shook it out. It had gold buttons and the Ashton Hotel crest. She held it up against his blue shirt.

'No.'

'What have we got to lose?'

'Our dignity?'

She laughed. 'Seriously, we lost that when we chased a photographer across south London.'

'Our privacy?'

'That's why you're wearing this uniform. They won't know it's you.'

'Someone will recognise me.'

'Do you look at wait staff?'

'I do, as it happens.'

Yes, Rowan was just that kind of person. Isabella tried to be, but knew she often fell short. She also knew that most people, whether they admitted it or not, did not.

'You do, but most people don't, and you know that. Besides, you have a beard now. You're utterly unrecognisable.'

'You recognised me,' he muttered.

I'd know you anywhere, she thought, looking into his whisky eyes and feeling herself falling into them.

In a year many things had changed—his demeanour was more serious, the beard, many of his expressions—but his eyes were the same. *I'd know you in another life. I'd know you in heaven.* She felt herself falling forward, shook herself and straightened.

No. Rowan was in her past and he had to stay there.

She turned to the shelves and the stash of uniforms stored there. Rummaging around, she found a white shirt, a starched white bib and finally a tie. She held the shirt up against him again. It looked about the right size. Now for some trousers.

'What choice do we have?' she said.

'You could go out there by yourself.'

She felt her insides crumple, but held her back straight, glad she was facing away from him.

She didn't do things alone. She was always part of a pair. A double act. It wasn't that she couldn't. At least, she didn't think so. She wanted him with her.

'We got in this together, we'll get out of it together.'

'Isn't it riskier?'

She located the trousers and searched for a pair that looked big enough for his tall frame. Her heart was racing as she neared the bottom of the pile without locating any, but at the bottom was finally a pair that looked large enough. She handed them to him.

'I don't know what I'm going to say to him. How I'm even going to find him,' she said.

'I can't talk to him for you. You have to do it yourself.'

'I know. But you can be close.'

Rowan lowered his brow and when he looked at her, her skin prickled. She'd said too much.

'And you can help me find him,' she added.

'I don't even know what he looks like,' Rowan pleaded.

'Old. White. Rich.'

'Like everyone in there.'

'I'll google him while you get changed.'

He still hesitated, looking at the clothes but not reaching for them.

You owe me this, she almost said. *You left me once. Don't leave me now.*

He will always leave. He doesn't love you enough to stay.

He shook his head. 'I don't think it's a good idea.'

'Of course it's not. I thought we were in this together. But I guess…'

You're not in this together. You haven't been a team since he left you three days before your wedding.

Rowan closed his eyes and breathed in through his nose. Then he sighed and said, 'Fine. You're right. It's my problem too. We are in this together.'

Her heart flipped a happy beat. 'Give me your phone and I'll show you what he looks like.'

Rowan handed her his phone and she searched for Liam Goldsworthy.

Sir Liam was exactly as she'd flippantly described to Rowan: old and white. On the other side of seventy, with short clipped grey hair and blue eyes that shined out from the photo she was looking at, bright and friendly.

Hopefully that friendliness was genuine and not a mirage.

Sir Liam owns a tabloid rag. Do you honestly think he's going to be co-operative?

What other choice did she have?

The sound of a belt unbuckling made her look up. Rowan had taken off his shoes and was now taking off his trousers. He was facing away from her, thankfully. She looked down, to his bare legs, his usual tight black shorts. His thigh muscles flexing as he pushed down his trousers and bent his legs.

She looked at the other wall, her heart fluttering against her ribs.

Was one little photo worth this? Standing in a too small and suddenly too warm room while her gorgeous ex stripped off?

'Um, when you're ready, I've found his photo,' she said to the wall.

'Just a sec,' he replied.

Knowing it was a bad idea, but not being able to help herself, she turned her head for a second. Seeing he was still facing the other way, she felt safer to fix her gaze on him. The trousers she'd found fitted him perfectly, but he did have one of those physiques. Tight across the seat and well fitted around his thighs. Her throat went dry as she admired him. He unbuttoned his blue shirt and she watched as he took his arms out and his muscles rippled beneath the surface of his taut, smooth skin. A swimmer's shoulders, even broader and firmer than in her memories. Her fingertips tingled as they recalled the smoothness of his skin under them. How she could trace patterns and words into his body for hours with her fingers, and her lips. Her mouth salivated with the memory of his taste.

What if the photos got out there? Sure, she'd upset everyone she loved most in the world, but she wouldn't have to be *here*. Watching this. Watching everything she'd lost, so close she could almost taste it. Taste him.

Luckily Rowan didn't turn as he reached for the white shirt, his muscles stretching, flexing and rippling again as he slid his long arms into it. Crisp white cotton slid over warm, pale skin. Sprinkled with just a few freckles. Smooth and entirely lickable.

He turned and showed her the shirt, holding out his arms and then, for good measure, doing another spin.

'You look good.' Her mouth was dry. Both understatements.

'Thanks, I think.' He folded his own trousers and shirt neatly, laying one on top of the other, and slid them onto a nearby shelf.

Isabella picked up a loose white tie and he stepped towards her. Instead of simply handing it to him, her hand looped it around his neck. She lifted his collar and slipped the fabric under. His Adam's apple bobbed with a deep gulp.

She adjusted the fabric and rested her palms against his shoulders, sliding them down to rest on his collarbone. She knew she should lift them away, she'd lingered too long, but his chest felt so good, so nice. His muscles tensed under her touch and, finally, she took her hands reluctantly away.

'I actually have no idea what I'm doing. I can't tie a half Windsor let alone one of these things,' she confessed and stepped back, head down.

''S okay,' he said, his voice rough. 'But there isn't a mirror. Could you please hold up the camera of my phone?'

'Good idea,' she said. Glad to be useful and glad to have an excuse to watch him weave and bend the fabric over and under itself in deft, practised moves as the fabric became a perfect bow tie.

Tie tied, he picked up the black jacket and shrugged it on.

'How do I look?'

'Honestly?'

Honestly, you always look hot. You couldn't not look hot. I want to rip those clothes right off you again and make love to you on this dusty floor.

But she didn't say that. She reminded herself that this was the very same man who had destroyed her trust in all men and happy endings, and turned away. The man who had changed his mind about her and their life together as soon as things began to get a little difficult. Isabella didn't care about Rowan's father's past and didn't see that Rowan should take it all so personally either. She wasn't even angry about the photos from Rowan's stag night; everyone knew the press loved to manufacture compromising situations for celebrities to get caught in. Isabella believed

Rowan was blameless and only trying to extract himself from the situation.

She had trusted him, forgiven him and for what? He'd left at the first complication. And if Rowan, the man she'd loved more than any other, had done that, how could she possibly trust anyone again?

A box on a nearby shelf caught her eye. She pulled a disposable face mask out of a box and handed it to him. 'Maybe put this on. Just in case.'

'I thought you said I was unrecognisable in the beard?'

'I was joking! Wear the mask.'

Confusion creased his face but he took it.

'Okay, show me what this guy looks like.'

She reopened to the photo of Sir Liam and handed him back his phone. 'The next one is with his wife.'

'So, he looks like every other middle-aged man who is here tonight.'

'Yep.'

While Rowan gathered his wallet and pulled on the borrowed jacket, Isabella contemplated sending a message to her sister.

She had no intention of telling Francesca everything, particularly not about all these 'getting stuck in confined spaces with her ex' shenanigans, but that didn't matter. Her sister would be worried.

Though Francesca would want answers to questions Isabella couldn't answer.

'Let's do this, then.' Rowan gently touched her shoulder, turning her then nudging her to the door. But Isabella stopped short of it, her hand in mid-air, not yet touching the doorknob.

'We need to go separately.'

'Definitely.'

'So I'll go, you'll follow.'

'I'm right behind you. I promise.'

Still she paused.

'I don't know what I'm going to say.'

'Ask him not to print it.'

'Just lead with that?'

'Well, butter him up a bit at least. Ask him how he enjoyed the coronation.'

'Lame.'

'I've got nothing else.'

'You're the clever one. What would you say to him if you were me?'

Rowan grasped her shoulders and turned her back to face him. 'You, Isabella di Marzano, Princess of Monterossa, are the smartest and most charming woman I've ever known. And the most self-assured.'

Maybe. But that was before I met you. Before everything changed. Before I began to doubt everything, including myself.

CHAPTER FIVE

ISABELLA STILL DIDN'T BUDGE. Rowan looked at his watch. It was after ten p.m. They had to get out there now and find the newspaper owner. He had no idea how long a coronation party would last. Maybe until after midnight? But how long would a newspaper owner party on? They couldn't take their chances.

'We need to get out there.'

'I know. But I still don't know what to say to him!'

What happened to the bright confident woman he'd known?

You did this.

He pushed the thought down. No. That wasn't so. Isabella was far better off without someone one like him. She'd been absolutely fine when he'd ended their engagement, calm, serene. She hadn't argued. She certainly hadn't cried. He didn't doubt that she cared for him, but the way she'd reacted so well to the break-up convinced him she would get over him soon.

The woman before him now was not the same woman. She was as beautiful and compelling, perhaps more so than a year ago. But something was missing.

'You can do this,' he said again. 'Just use your famous charm.'

'My *famous* charm?' She smiled and dipped her head, lifted her gaze.

His insides flipped. '*That* charm.'

'I wasn't trying to be charming.' She still looked up at him through fluttering lashes.

'Regardless, it comes naturally to you.'

'And now?' She lifted a manicured hand and removed some non-existent fluff from his lapel. When she removed her hand the slide of one finger brushed ever so gently under his chin and his throat closed over. He was never entering a small room alone with her again.

'Now you know you're being charming.' His throat closed over.

'Flirting. It's not exactly the same thing.'

'I think for this evening's purposes we shouldn't quibble with semantics. Do what needs to be done.'

'I can't flirt with Sir Liam! He's married.' As she spoke, she placed her hand on Rowan's shoulder.

'I wasn't saying you should flirt, I said you should be charming.'

'Where's the line between being charming and flirting?'

'I think it's like obscenity or art—you know it when you see it.' He was pretty sure he was looking at that line right now. They were standing closer than ever, but he wasn't sure if she'd stepped forward or if he had. They seemed to have exhausted all the air in the room and his head spun. Common sense must have been as scarce as the oxygen and he said, 'You're looking so beautiful tonight, I'm sure if you just walk up to him he'd do anything you ask.' His voice was rough but he was powerless to change it. He couldn't get enough air into his lungs.

'Now who's flirting with who?' Her voice was as ragged as his.

Isabella's dress was fitted to her curves, the neckline was low and, not for the first time that night, he forced himself to look into her soft hazel eyes and away from her supple cleavage, shown to perfection by the cut of the dress. Their bodies moved even closer and by instinct he lifted his hand to her waist, the beading of her dress a little rough against the silk. He might have been holding her body, but he was also holding her at a safe distance from himself. A safe distance.

You think this distance is safe?

The voice in the back of his head squawked with laughter. Nothing about this moment was safe.

'Just go out there, introduce yourself. People love meeting a princess, you know that.'

'Even in a room full of other princesses and duchesses?'

He couldn't believe how insecure she sounded. *You did this.*

No. Isabella was fine without him.

She let out a deep sigh that he felt in his gut.

'There's a lot riding on it. For both of us. I want this to work.'

'I know. Ask him how his night has been. And then ask him not to print the photographs. I for one would…'

He closed his eyes. It was too much. This room, this moment, Isabella standing so close to him, smelling like Monterossa, long nights and languid, lazy mornings.

'You for one would?'

'Do anything you asked.' He exhaled and pulled her closer.

'Anything?' Her voice was as whisper thin as his resolve.

'Anything.'

A glimpse of her tongue touching her top lip was all it took to send him back twelve months, back to before the wedding, before everything about his family came out. Back to the time he could tighten his arms around her, pull her close and press his mouth against hers whenever he wanted.

As he did now. He heard her take in a breath of air sharply as his body collapsed into her, his mouth opened, his arms pulled her against him. He tasted her, trembled as her tongue slid against his, erasing a year of self-control in an instant. His body tightened, his head exploded. The inevitable conclusion to this situation. He was powerless in her arms, lost, adrift. He devoured her like a starving man.

And then she was gone. Air where her body had been.

'Not everything,' she panted.

No. Because while it was easy to give her this, he couldn't give her a future.

The guilt crashed over him again, hot and bitter, with no cure.

'I'm so sorry, I shouldn't have—'

'I guess we've established at least I can still get your attention.' She looked at the ground and drew a circle on the floor with one of her red shoes.

'Isabella, I'm sorry. I shouldn't have...'

She shook her head. 'It takes two, but I guess we've established where the line between charming and flirting is. I won't try that with Sir Liam.'

'Isabella...' He tried to speak again but couldn't find the words. His brain kept freezing as soon as he said her name.

'I know you're sorry. I know you wish things

could be different. I know you think you can't change things,' she said.

Her choice of words snagged in his muddled brain. 'Of course I wish things were different.'

I know you think you can't change things.

Of course he couldn't change things! No one could change the fact she was a princess and he was a school dropout who couldn't even manage to keep himself and his family out of the papers. The whole world could see he wasn't good enough for her.

'I wish things were different, but I can't change the world. We are who we are.'

'Of course,' she said. But it was clear she wasn't buying it. If she wanted someone to change the world then she was definitely stuck in a small room with the wrong man. 'Rowan, we can't talk about this now. We need to get out there.'

'So go,' he said. The clock was ticking. For all they knew, Sir Liam might have left the party already.

She nodded, but still looked unsure.

You did this.

He nudged her chin up with his index finger and took her gaze in his. His insides tumbled and twisted like the most daring of acrobats. How did she not realise how amazing she was?

'Walking away from you was the hardest thing I've ever done in my life and I seriously doubt any man, particularly one who has probably enjoyed quite a few post-coronation champagnes, could seriously say no to you.'

She smiled but it seemed as though she was trembling.

Isabella turned and this time she couldn't grab the doorknob fast enough.

'You should wait a few minutes. The ballroom is that way,' she said and waved her hand, but neither of them were in a state to be paying attention to directions at this point. He could hardly have sworn which way was up and which was down, his head still spinning from the kiss.

'Good luck,' he said as she slipped out of the door, closing it behind her.

Rowan took the moment to compose himself.

You kissed her? What were you thinking?

He had been thinking of the palace in Monterossa, of The Ritz, of all the times they had been alone together. Of all the moments they had shared. He had *not* been thinking of self-preservation.

If Isabella was uncertain about their mission, then Rowan was positively pessimistic. Not only was this mission most likely futile, but it was also downright risky. He knew hotels like this were meant to have a 'no photography' policy but hundreds of people might see them. And it only took one to tattle.

Rowan James sneaks into Duke's coronation party to woo royal ex!

The potential headline made him shiver and the bow tie tightened like a noose around his neck. He slipped the face mask she had given him over his mouth and nose.

If only he'd put that on five minutes earlier.

That he shouldn't have kissed Isabella was a no-brainer. It had shaken him and clearly surprised her, further muddying all the waters between them.

He'd never denied that he still had feelings for her, he'd just realised that those feelings were not strong enough to make way for everything else.

It's just the fact that you were close together, reassuring her that she can do this. It was a blip, a natural mistake. Forgive yourself.

It didn't mean anything.

They were not getting back together. Another reason it was imperative he got out into this party and helped her track down Sir Liam.

Rowan opened the door slowly and looked out into a warren of narrow hallways leading in all directions. Left, he decided, though wished he had something to stick on the door so he'd be able to find his clothes again. Or better yet, a pocketful of breadcrumbs to make a trail back.

The hotel was like many Mayfair buildings, several hundred years old and, even though it had been recently remodelled, it had been renovated to look as though Queen Victoria were still the monarch. The narrow back corridors were for the servants, which should have made him feel more comfortable but when one of the staff rushed past him, he gave Rowan a filthy look.

If you're dressed like the staff you need to act like it!

Rowan nodded and hurried away. He needed a tray of glasses to carry as soon as possible.

Luckily, he'd always identified more closely with the staff at these events than he had with any of the guests. Aristocrats. Royalty. Old money. Rowan might be just as rich as many of the people here, even more so, but he was not of this world. He was from a flat across the river, which his family could only afford with the help of the housing benefit.

At the end of the corridor was half a flight of stairs and at the top of the stairs the noise of the party was loudest. He walked up the stairs, pushed open the door at the top and found himself in a large room.

He'd been to a few charity galas in his time and this was a lot like one of those. The room was crowded with almost identical-looking people: the men wore dark suits, the women dressed conservatively in blacks and dark blues. The most daring wore silver, or perhaps a deep purple. He could easily spot Isabella in her red ensemble as soon as he entered the room. Like a beacon.

Or perhaps that was simply because he could spot her in any crowd. Even if the face mask had been covering his eyes he'd still have had a way of knowing Isabella was nearby. The air would feel different. His bones would know.

Worse than that, other people always noticed her. Even if they hadn't shared a history, he would have seen her. A stand-out beauty.

As Rowan stood at the door, frozen, another woman, one dressed in the same black and white get-up as him, stared at him. Not with the annoyed look of the other man but with a 'Who the hell are you?' look.

He nodded at the woman. 'Busy night, hey?' he said, and she walked away shaking her own head. Hopefully she wasn't heading off to find someone with the authority to kick him out.

He might have been better off just coming to the party as himself.

Don't be silly. Everyone knows that Rowan James doesn't belong at a party like this.

He was a waiter. He needed to act like one.

With his heart rate increasing, he decided that as the newest member of staff he should collect empty glasses. He didn't need to know where to take them, as long as it looked as though he was moving around the room.

He weaved his way through the crowd, trying simultaneously to search for empty glasses and Sir Liam, while also keeping his gaze down.

A challenge at the best of times.

As he approached the doorway across from the

one he'd come in, his stomach fell. There was a whole other room, a much larger one, where people were dancing.

Damn.

He spotted a bar. The two men behind it were too busy preparing drinks to notice him slip in behind them and pick up an empty black tray. Good, he felt better. If anything he could use it to cover his face. Rowan had a flashback to the time before his business has taken off, working in his mother's pub. His mother always said it was fortunate he came up with the idea for the app because his ability to carry a tray of drinks left something to be desired.

'What are you doing just standing there? Those glasses need clearing.'

The man looked Rowan up and down.

'Yes, sir,' Rowan said before ducking away to search for some empty glasses to put on his empty tray.

The situation encapsulated his relationship with Isabella in a nutshell. She was swirling around with royalty and aristocracy, looking elegant and jaw-droopingly gorgeous. Charming everyone in her path.

And he was in a waiter's uniform. Collecting empty glasses. Pretending to be someone he was not.

Rowan kept his head down and picked up empty glasses. How would he know when Isabella had been successful? They should have been coming up with a better plan instead of kissing, he thought as he made his way around the edge of the room.

He balanced a final champagne flute on the tray and turned to head back to the bar. A man walked past him quickly and gesticulating, requiring Rowan to step back suddenly, causing him to tip the precariously balanced tray to one side.

The noise of shattering glass made everyone around him jump.

This was bad. Very bad. His face was burning under the mask and sweat began to gather on his forehead.

'What on earth?'

It was the man who had viewed him suspiciously in the corridor earlier.

'I'll clean it up.' He almost added, 'And of course I'll pay.' An instinct that thankfully he kept to himself.

'You bet you will.'

Rowan bent down and stacked the tray with the chunks of glass, thankful most were in large pieces, not shattered into sharp shards. Another man crouched down next to him and began helping. He was wearing a suit, but of a far finer fabric than the rough jackets given to the staff. Rowan looked at the man's face. Grey hair, blue eyes. It was Sir Liam.

Worse still, the man looked into Rowan's face and his eyes widened with recognition.

Damn!

You were never good enough, but you really messed things up with her. Royally.

He couldn't even laugh at his own joke.

'I can manage, thank you, sir,' Rowan said, but Sir Liam kept stacking glass onto the tray. Rowan kept his eyes down until the tray was finally full and no pieces remained. He nodded to Sir Liam without making eye contact and turned away.

Now, while he was carrying a tray of broken glass, he had to find Isabella, and point her in the direction of the commotion he'd just caused.

The last time he'd spotted Isabella's red dress she'd been in the first room. He had to get to her, direct her to the larger room with the dancing.

Rowan was headed in that direction when he was stopped by a hand on his shoulder, heavy, insistent.

'May I have a word?' said the deep voice belonging to it.

Isabella made her way through the party, head spinning. She could hardly focus on the faces around her. Her lips were still sensitive from the kiss Rowan had given her in the storeroom. It had been like a summer shower—unexpected, heavy and very brief. And it had left the air around her steamy afterwards.

He'd apologised, but she had goaded him into it, with all her talk of flirting. For a moment, locked away from the rest of the world, it was almost as though she'd forgotten they had broken up. Like one of those dreams she kept on having in which they were still together, only to wake up and be cruelly reminded all over again that she was alone.

Abandoned.

She'd pushed him into it, just as she'd pushed him into the engagement. Thinking only of herself, her own desires. She had to compartmentalise.

It was a strategy she'd practised many times over the past year to get herself through engagements, or even dinner with her parents, when all she really wanted to do was curl up in bed, cover her face with a duvet and cry.

Compartmentalise. Smile serenely. Push it down.

The kiss, and analysing its implications, or even reliving its magnificence, had to wait until she'd found Sir Liam.

The crowd at the party had thinned since she'd been here three hours earlier, but the average age of the guests hadn't decreased at all. She was still likely to be one of the only people under thirty. Heaven knew how her mother thought she'd find someone suitable to marry here.

These are your type of people. People who understand your family and way of life.

But walking through the crowd, she didn't feel as though she belonged at all. She felt as if she were floating to one side of them all. They didn't understand what it was like to be her. Very few people in the world really understood. Even the two people in the world she was closest to didn't understand at all. One had abandoned her. And the other would move on to a new life shortly.

The fact that neither of them intended to hurt her didn't lessen her pain one little bit. Rowan had chosen to protect his family and friends. Francesca would only do that which was her destiny.

But they were still leaving her.

Isabella couldn't see Sir Liam anywhere. Or Rowan for that matter. Certain Sir Liam was not in the first room, she picked up her pace and moved to the next. She had to stop the photograph being published.

Her family hadn't been rocked by the kind of scandals other royal families had faced but her parents had made her and her sister well aware of them.

'It's always best to learn from the mistakes of others than to make them yourself,' her father often said.

This potential scandal was hardly on the scale of some scandals but she would disappoint her parents, on what was meant to be her sister's chance to show them that she was ready to represent Monterossa. With her father still in hospital, it would embarrass her family when they needed it least.

She sighed.

Compartmentalise. Smile.

This next room was a lounge, filled with small tables and chairs. She surveyed the room, looking for Sir Liam. But also for Rowan.

She had no luck with either and moved on to the next. The ballroom was three times the size of the two rooms she'd already come through, but with ten times as many people. She began her circuit of the room, smiling and nodding at those who she recognised, or at those who recognised her.

The band was still playing, a mixture of swing and jazz, the sort of thing she always heard at these sorts of parties and never anywhere else. They paused at the end of a song and she heard it. Shattering glass. She, like everyone in the room, turned to the sound of the commotion.

Damn.

There was Sir Liam, but worse than that. He was crouched on the floor next to a man picking up the glass. A man she'd recognise anywhere.

And they were speaking to one another! What if he recognised Rowan? He was supposed to stay inconspicuous, yet here he was dropping glasses and speaking to their target.

Though, she supposed, the chances of Rowan staying inconspicuous anywhere were always low, even before he'd been engaged to a princess and the world knew his face. His face had always been handsome, his figure always striking.

He's dressed as a waiter, bearded and wearing a mask. No one will recognise him.

She no longer believed the pep talk she'd given him. This was a ridiculous plan. She needed to separate Sir Liam from Rowan, talk to him and get both her and Rowan out of the party as soon as possible.

By the time Isabella had reached that side of the room, Rowan had disappeared. Her heart beat faster with each step.

'Even if you aren't confident, you need to give the impression that you are.'

Words her mother had said to her and Francesca over and over again.

'Pretend you're in a movie, and the world is your stage.'

Something that was easier for a trained actress to espouse.

Start with the wife.

She wasn't sure why or even where the thought came from, but it seemed like a natural way to ease herself into their conversation. She stood to one side of Lady Goldsworthy, a friendly looking woman who was clutching a glass of red wine and laughing animatedly with the woman next

to her. This was good. Older women were more
practical, less spooked by royalty. She caught
Lady Goldsworthy's eye and smiled. The woman
smiled back. The other woman, curious about
what had captured her companion's attention, also
turned and, noticing Isabella, also smiled. 'Your
Highness.'

'Hello,' Isabella began, because there was no
better way to begin a conversation. 'Are you having a nice evening?'

'Oh, yes, it's been lovely.'

They chatted about the party and the coronation earlier that day. Lady Goldsworthy poured
Isabella a glass of their wine and Isabella almost
forgot her mission.

The sound of the women's laughter attracted
Sir Liam's attention and Isabella met his eye.

'Your Highness,' he said as he joined them.

At least he knew who she was. That was a start.

'The Princess was just telling us what the
Prime Minister was overheard saying at the coronation.'

'You've had a good day, then, Your Highness?'
Sir Liam smiled at her knowingly. He *had* recognised Rowan! This was very bad.

Next time she would listen to Francesca when
she told her a plan was risky.

'Yes,' she said, not trusting her voice to stay
even.

'And your sister?'

'She's around here somewhere.' Isabella waved her hand in the air and pretended to search the dance floor for her sister.

'She's probably out there dancing,' said Lady Goldsworthy. 'You young things should be on the dance floor, not talking to the old folks.'

'I agree. But I don't think for a second that any of you are old. You should join me.'

Lady Goldsworthy laughed. 'Oh, not me.'

'Sir Liam?' Isabella asked. 'Would you do me the honour?'

His wife chuckled and Sir Liam hesitated for a moment before his wife said, 'Go on!'

And that was how Liam Goldsworthy, owner of *The Truth*, happened to take Isabella's hand and lead her onto the dance floor at the Ashton.

She hoped Rowan was somewhere in the room watching. They'd done it!

Well, not quite yet. She'd found him and got him alone but still had to ask him not to print the photograph.

You're looking so beautiful tonight I'm sure if you just walk up to him he'd do anything you ask.

'Are you having a good night?' he asked.

'I'm having an interesting night,' she replied truthfully.

He chuckled. 'The very best kind.'

'Yes, well, I'm glad you agree. I think yours might be about to become even more interesting.'

He narrowed his eyes and studied her. It felt strangely like dancing with her grandfather.

'Have you ever had a relationship go wrong? End in heartbreak?' she asked.

'Why do you ask?'

'Have you?'

He nodded.

'And it isn't nice, is it?'

He shook his head.

'Well, it's a hundred times worse when the entire world knows and is speculating about it and making assumptions and judging you. And you can't even get out of bed.'

'I'll have to take your word for it.' He cleared his throat.

'So…'

Just ask him!

'Has this got anything to do with the fact that your ex-fiancé is here tonight?'

'What?' she spluttered.

'You didn't know? For some reason he's here as a waiter, but not doing a very good job of it. I think he might be about to be fired.'

'You recognised him?'

'Was I not meant to?'

Isabella grimaced.

'Are you back together?'

'No,' she said but knew her face was turning red.

It was just a kiss, a mistake, it didn't mean anything. He didn't want to marry a princess. They were definitely *not* back together.

'Yet, he's here tonight.'

'About that.'

'Yes?'

'We ran into one another, earlier. At another place. But accidentally, it wasn't planned. We haven't seen one another since...'

'Since he broke it off?' Sir Liam prompted.

He seemed very kind and understanding. He would hear her out and agree to her request.

'Yes, and we were talking and trying not to be seen because, well...'

'You wanted privacy.'

'Exactly. But we were seen and photographed. But we're not back together.'

'You said that. Where are you going with this?'

'The photograph was of us coming out of a storeroom together. Nothing happened, but we were in a cupboard together. And he had his arm around me. And the photographer, a pap, sold the pictures to one of your papers.'

'Ah. And you don't want them printed.'

'Yes, that's it! Could you, please, as a favour, please not print them?'

'I don't make editorial decisions.'

'Not usually, but you can in special circumstances.'

'That's true. But what was really so bad about this photo? What's the big deal?' Liam Goldsworthy seemed like a decent man, and he had a very nice wife, so she decided honesty was the best policy.

'Rowan left me because of the press intrusion in his life, but mostly his family and friends'. As much as that broke my heart, I do understand it and I want to respect his wishes.'

'He's a grown man, and a successful one at that. I'm sure he can handle publicity.'

'But his family shouldn't have to. At least, not the kind of negative and hurtful attention they were subjected to. People telling their secrets, interfering with their lives.'

Sir Liam sighed. 'It's the price of public life.'

This man owns newspapers! What were you thinking asking him not to print a picture that will surely sell more papers? She needed to try a different angle.

'But it isn't just that. I don't want my father to see the photos.'

'He's been unwell?'

'Yes, very. That's why Francesca and I are here in the first place. I wouldn't want to upset him. Or my mother. That's really why I don't want the photos being published. It will embarrass my family and I want to avoid any more heartache for them.'

'I see.' He nodded and for the first time in hours Isabella felt lighter. He would agree not to publish! It would all be okay!

'I will ask my editor not to publish the photographs of you and Rowan James.'

'Oh, thank you, thank you!'

'Provided…'

Provided you pay me. Provide you have lunch with my wife… Provided…

'Provided you call my editor before seven a.m. and agree to do an exclusive interview with the paper instead.'

'Me? An exclusive interview?' She could do that. She would have much more control of the narrative this way. It would still be okay.

'You *and* him.'

'Rowan?'

'Yes. Both of you. Together. With all topics on the table. I'm not just going to tell my editors to give up photos like that, without something in return. Think of it as a way to put your side of the story out there. Some of the things you just told me. Though you won't have to mention what you were doing at that bar.'

'I… I'd have to talk to Rowan.'

'Of course. I don't require an answer now. My editor's name is Karl Brown. Call the paper before seven.'

He released his hold on her, leaving her unsteady as the other dancers whirled around her.

'Thank you, I appreciate it,' she said.

Liam made his way back to his wife, clearly recognising their transaction was over.

She had to find Rowan. And quickly.

Isabella spied a clock on the wall. It was nearly eleven. She had eight hours to convince him to tell his story to the press. She already knew that she wanted to accept Sir Liam's offer, but would Rowan, who guarded his privacy so closely, see that it was the best choice? She wasn't sure.

The last time she'd seen him he'd been carrying a tray full of broken glass to the back of the ballroom, so she went in that general direction now.

They'd have to leave out the back. The front door was still not an option, not with Rowan and he was her ride, not to mention still her only chance of stopping publication of the photo.

An interview.

Together.

She shivered.

This night just kept getting worse.

CHAPTER SIX

IT WAS ALL OVER.

Even if the photo of him and Isabella sneaking out of a cupboard wasn't published, a headline saying that he'd dressed as a waiter to sneak into the Duke's party probably would be.

What would be the consequences? Would he be charged with trespass? Fined? He wanted to throw up. Whatever the legal consequences were they paled into comparison with the ones that would follow if news of this got out. So much for keeping a low profile.

He needed an excuse, and fast.

'Come with me this way,' said the voice again.

Good. Hopefully they would go somewhere private. Rowan hated bribery and corruption but what would it take to get this man to stay silent?

'How about I just leave and we—?'

'Leave? The broken glass has to go out to the utility room. I don't know where you think you're taking it.'

'I… Ah…' Rowan added and looked properly at the owner of the voice for the first time.

'Have I seen you before?' the man asked.

'No, this is my first night here. You needed extra staff. I've come from…' *Think! Think!* 'The Duke's own household.'

'Of course, sorry, you don't know your way around.'

'I have no idea where I'm going,' Rowan said truthfully. 'And I would be very grateful if you could point me towards a broom.'

The man led him out of a different door and into more back passages and to a room with rubbish bins and cleaning products.

'Thank you, I think I'm all right from here,' Rowan said to the man.

'Good.' The man turned and Rowan exhaled.

But then the man turned back and studied him. Rowan's face turned hot under the mask. 'Most of us are going out for a drink after this is all over, if you want to join us?'

'A drink would be great. It's been quite a night.'

'Indeed.'

Finally the man turned and left.

Rowan rested his head against the wall and took some, deep steadying breaths. His limbs tingled from the adrenaline coursing through them. They needed to leave!

When his heart rate had returned to close to normal levels he disposed of the glass and searched for something with which to clean up the rest of the mess. As much as he wanted to slip out of the nearest door, he had to get back out there, find Isabella and point her to Sir Liam. His disguise was not going to work for much longer. For starters, the face mask was beginning to stick to his face with all the sweating that last encounter had caused. He spied another box of face masks, took another two and pocketed them.

At least with a broom he looked as though he had a purpose. With a deep breath he ventured back out to the ballroom.

Sir Liam was no longer anywhere to be seen. Great.

A waiter walked past him with a tray of full champagne flutes and he had to stop himself from grabbing one.

Once you find Isabella you can go to the nearest pub and order several Scotches neat.

The thought spurred him on. He went back to the place he thought he had dropped the glass and swept it up slowly. If he stayed in one spot, she might find him.

He took as long as he thought he possibly could sweeping the section of the floor but still Isabella did not return. Just when he was about to leave a flash of red caught his eye. Without making eye contact with her, he walked in her direction. Eventually she stepped into a corridor leading away from the ballroom. He followed.

'We have to get out of here,' she whispered.

He nodded. 'I just need to get my clothes.'

'No time. Sir Liam knows you're here.'

'Damn. I was worried about that.'

'So we have to leave *now*.'

'What did he say?'

'Later. Come.'

She tugged his arm and pulled him down the corridor. It was narrow and led off to another maze of hallways.

'I need to get back to my clothes.'

'Were you very attached to them?'

'I'd like to keep them. Besides, I can't keep walking around dressed like the staff. They keep getting angry at me. I'm a terrible waiter, as it happens.'

'I'll buy you some new ones. We have to go. No. Wait.'

Isabella spun him towards her, grabbed the lapels of his jacket and tugged it over his shoulders and off his arms. She balled it up and tossed it behind a large pot plant nearby.

'There, now you just look like a badly dressed guest. Let's go.'

But before they could take another step the sound of laughter floated down the hallway, behind them.

They could not be seen together like this! He grabbed her hand and was momentarily stilled by the firmness of her grip, the easy fit of her hand in his and the sensations distractingly skittering up his arm. A laugh down the corridor brought him back to the present and he pulled Isabella away from the voices. This part of the hotel was no less of a maze than the rest but around two more corners they saw a sign for a fire exit. He looked at her. 'Out here?'

'It's as good a door as any.'

He pushed on the heavy door it and it gave.

Unfortunately at the same time his ears began to sting with the sound of a large, urgent alarm.

'Ahh, there's a fire!' she said.

At least that was what he thought she said over the noise.

No.

There wasn't a fire. Just an alarm. One he had just set off.

'Damn.'

He pulled the door closed quickly but the noise continued.

'What are you doing?' she asked.

'I set off the alarm.'

'Yes, so now we really have to go.'

He pushed the door all the way open and seconds later they were out into the fresh night air. The problem was that within moments other people were emerging out into the street as well. They had exited onto a side street that was busier than the laneway where he'd left his bike, which wasn't ideal, but, even worse, they couldn't get back to his bike without passing all the people that were now streaming out of another nearby door.

They looked at one another. Without speaking, they both inclined their heads towards another laneway, nodded and then walked as quickly as they could away from the Ashton, Sir Liam, Rowan's clothes and his Vespa.

They walked in since down the deserted passageway. Next to him he felt Isabella trembling. Was she frightened, crying? He wanted to turn and check on her but it was more important that they got well out of the way of the other people.

When he was satisfied they were at least two blocks away and the crowds had thinned, he ducked into a doorway and pulled her in with him. She was trembling.

With laughter.

'Oh, my God. You set the alarm off. Each time I think this night can't get worse, it does.'

Tears streamed down her face and she was trying hard not to throw her head back and laugh as loudly as she could.

'It's not funny. It's stressful.'

Not to mention the stress of the fact that I kissed you back there. That I'm still holding your hand in mine.

Rowan untangled his fingers from hers and let her hand drop.

'It's funny because it's awful. I can still hear that alarm. We've ruined that party.'

'Please tell me you spoke to him?'

'I did. Thanks to you and your tray-dropping trick.'

'It wasn't a trick, it was an accident. What did he say?'

'He agreed not to publish the photos.'

'Great!' Rowan wrapped his arms around her waist, picked her up and twirled her around.

'Put me down.' She slapped his arm. 'It's not that simple.'

'I guess it was too much to hope for.'

'But it's okay. He won't publish the photos if we agree to an interview with the paper.'

'You?'

'Both of us.'

'Oh.'

'Together. And we have to let his editor know by seven a.m. I think we should do it. We can choose what we say, and we'll have much more control over this whole situation. And then no one will find out about the cupboard. Or Twilight.'

Rowan shook his head. 'They'll ask all about my family.'

'And it's your chance to set the record straight. Better that you answer the questions than that they go through your parents' rubbish.'

She had a point, but his gut still said no. Doing an interview together would prompt questions about their relationship. How and why it ended. How he *felt* about it. It would be a lose-lose situation. He couldn't refuse to answer the questions, but how could he answer every question with absolute truth? Do you miss her? Do you still have feelings for her? Why did you really break up with her? No. A photo would be preferable. It wasn't even that bad. So what if they were together? In a small space? Nothing had happened.

'No. The photo isn't great, but it's far better than a tell-all interview!'

'We don't actually tell them everything. We decide how we answer the questions. The interview is a far better option.'

'No, letting the photo out is the best thing to do.'

For you.

For Isabella it would not be. It would upset her parents, embarrass her family.

'We should go somewhere and talk properly.'

'I agree, but where?'

They turned back to the Ashton but knew the streets around it would still be teeming with the people who had had to evacuate the party. It was too risky to go back for his bike.

'We walk somewhere.'

'Where? We can't go to my hotel. If you come in with me, Francesca could find out.'

'No, but we can go to mine.'

'You're staying in a hotel?'

'Yes. I sold my town house.'

'What? But you loved it.'

He had loved it. He could have afforded to keep it when he'd relocated to the States but he'd preferred to let it go. As he had with so many things that reminded him of Isabella.

It was simply easier that way.

'I'm staying at a hotel,' he repeated, avoiding answering her question.

'Near here?' she said hopefully.

'It's a walk.'

'Does that mean a long one or a short one?'

He looked down at her feet. He could manage but stilettos were not designed for a cross-city hike.

'I think it's too risky to get a cab,' he said.

'I don't think we could even if we wanted to.'

The street where they were was quiet. If they went towards the main streets and the traffic they would run into the crowds.

'I can manage. Just come over here for a moment.' She opened her small bag and pulled out something. He watched, amazed, as she unfolded a pair of what looked like ballet slippers.

'What?'

'Spare shoes. For just this sort of thing.' She handed him her bag and the spare shoes and he watched while she braced herself against a nearby wall and tugged off her stilettos.

'You can walk in these?'

'I mean, I probably wouldn't do the Camino de Santiago trail in them, but they'll do for a walk across London.' When she was done changing her shoes she gave a little bounce and took back her bag and high heels, which she hooked under a finger. 'Let's go.'

'You always have those?'

'Not always, but Francesca broke a heel once so we've tried to carry some ever since. Just in case. She has the hairbrush.'

'Pardon?'

'She has the hairbrush in her bag. And the tampons. We each have our own lipstick.'

'I don't understand.'

'As long as we're together, we're covered. And we don't both need to carry heaps of stuff around.'

'You've always done this?' How did he not know?

'Pretty much. When you're always together, it's easier.'

Like a married couple, he thought, but fortunately stopped himself from saying it aloud.

Another reason why breaking off their engagement was a good thing. He'd only get in the way of what she had with her sister.

'I hope she doesn't need the emergency shoes,' Isabella mused.

'Where do you think she is?'

'Hopefully having fun and not worried about me.'

'She will be though. Shouldn't you call her?'

'Not until I've fixed this. I can't even begin to

explain to her where I am until I've sorted this. She'll be fine.'

He wasn't sure if Isabella was trying to convince him or herself.

'Lead on.'

'I'm back across the river. Maybe thirty minutes away?'

'Easy.'

'Oh, and here, I got us these,' he said, handing her one of the two face masks he'd taken from the Ashton.

'Great, at least something has gone right,' she said.

He shook his head. Nothing about this evening had gone right as far as he was concerned.

The back streets of Whitehall were much quieter than Mayfair and St James's, which had hundreds of revellers still pouring down the Mall and around St James's Park. She let Rowan lead the way as he was far more familiar with the area than she was and he knew the right streets to detour down.

'I'm sorry, I'm not taking the direct route.'

'I understand, we're avoiding people. I appreciate it, thank you.'

It wasn't until Westminster Abbey appeared in front of her that she realised where she was. It was all lit up with gold and white lights. Its gothic facade looked almost magical.

'Is it always this pretty? I don't remember it being like this,' she said.

'They have special lights for the coronation. It's quite something, isn't it?'

Less than twenty-four hours ago she'd walked through the great arch of the west door, Francesca by her side. The world's media looking on.

Francesca had stopped at the door, Isabella remembered, and she had looked up at all the stone figures carved around them. Isabella had followed suit, but couldn't see what Francesca was looking at.

'What must it feel like? To be one of the handful of men and women who have walked through those doors in the last thousand years, to be crowned? I wonder what the crown feels like when they place it on your head,' Francesca had said softly.

Isabella had noticed the line of guests stall behind them. This had not been the moment for Francesca's existential crisis, so Isabella had said, 'Heavy, I imagine,' and tugged her sister gently down the main aisle of the abbey, which had been buzzing with the voices of several thousand people.

She'd forgotten that moment, distracted by all the people and the spectacle of the coronation. But she remembered it now. She'd been focusing on what her sister's ascension would mean for her and her life, but hadn't let herself wonder what Francesca could be going through with their father's ill health hanging over them.

'I need to call Francesca.'

'Good idea.'

Isabella plonked herself down on a nearby bench. She put down her shoes, took out her phone and turned it on. There were several missed calls and at least a dozen messages from Francesca, each getting more frantic than the last.

Where are you?

Seriously?

I'm not your mother but I need to know you're okay.

Call me!!!

Isabella groaned. It was too much to hope that Francesca wouldn't be worried about her and would just go on enjoying her night. This was even one more mistake to add to the increasingly long list she was compiling this evening. She had only wanted to fix this mess before she called Francesca, she should have got in touch much earlier. Shouldn't have been so distracted by Rowan. And hugging him on the Vespa. Or watching him get changed.

She dialled Francesca, but she didn't pick up.

When the voicemail kicked in Isabella said, 'I'm so sorry, so so sorry. But I'm okay. I'll be back soon.'

Back soon? Really, Isabella, it's nearly midnight and you're on your way to Rowan's hotel room!

Yes.

Back soon.

They'd have something to eat and drink, she'd convince him to do the interview and then she'd call a car to come and get her.

Back to her hotel in plenty of time for her midday flight.

'Was it amazing? The coronation?' Rowan asked.

Even though it was only earlier that day, it felt like weeks ago. 'Yes, but it was also tiring. Don't laugh. You have to sit properly for six hours in case a camera pans over you.'

And they were always on the lookout for that sort of thing. An eye roll, a scratch of your nose or a badly timed laugh. Anything to find fault in. Any reason to mention that it was a good thing she was the spare princess.

'Let's get going, then.' He held out a hand to help her up and she looked at it. How she wanted to take it and hold it and pull herself into him for one big hug. Just an embrace of comfort, nothing more. Her emotions had been through the wringer over the past few hours.

But if she let herself take a comforting hug, she'd want more. It would be a very slippery slope that she would be powerless to stop herself sliding down. She stood and nodded.

You can do this on your own.

'It would probably be quicker to go across Westminster Bridge but that can be quite busy. Especially with all the tourists along the South Bank. I suggest we go along the Embankment and across Waterloo.'

She followed him until they reached the Thames and the city opened up in front of them. Isabella let herself exhale. It was getting close to midnight, but the lights of the city had been left on and the skyline glowed with many colours.

Even if they were coming the long way, it was something to walk along the Thames at night. The London Eye was to their right and also appeared to be lit up especially for the coronation. They soon approached the bend in the river and the rest of the skyline revealed itself to them.

Isabella walked to the ledge overlooking the river and leant on it, resting her elbows on the stone and looking around. From this vantage point you could see upstream to Westminster Bridge. Downstream were the other bridges and the shiny new buildings on the South Bank.

Only when she stopped did she realise they had set off in such a hurry she hadn't picked up her shoes.

'Damn. I left my shoes behind at the abbey.'

'Oh, no. You don't want to go back, do you?'

'No way. Your clothes, my shoes. I hope someone with the right size foot finds them and likes them.'

He laughed.

The shoes were lovely, but replaceable. Their reputations were not.

They still hadn't talked properly about Sir Liam's offer, and she sensed they were not going to agree.

'No one can hear us now. What exactly did he say?' Rowan asked.

'He wants something in return. Which we should have guessed.'

It had been a brief exchange, and she hadn't got anything in writing, but what choice did she have? She hardly had the best negotiating position.

'I think an interview is preferable. We have more control, we don't need to answer questions we don't want to. And most important of all, no one will know that Francesca and I left the Duke's party or that you are in London for Will's wedding.'

'I've thought that through. Either way I'm going to leave London as soon as I can. It's too risky to go to the wedding.'

'Rowan, no. That's not right either. They want you there.'

'No, the only important people at that wedding

are Will and Lucy. I've caused them both enough grief; I'm not going to ruin their big day as well. That wouldn't be fair.'

When the photos from Rowan's stag night had been published, Will had been one of the most affected. Social media had been splashed with photos of Will standing very close to two scantily clad women, everyone looking intoxicated.

Nothing had happened, but it had looked bad and Lucy had been understandably very upset. Isabella didn't know all the details as she'd been weathering her own personal crisis at the time, but she understood that for a few days it had seemed as though Will and Lucy's relationship might not survive.

It had though, and hopefully they were stronger for it, but what they had gone through had hurt them. And it wasn't their fault.

But it wasn't Rowan's either.

'You can't stop living your life because of an inconvenience.'

He rounded on her. 'It's more than an inconvenience—it's harassment. I can handle it, but those around me shouldn't have to.'

It took all of Isabella's restraint not to say, 'Easy for you to say. I don't get a choice.'

As usual, she swallowed her true feelings down and instead she said as calmly as she could, 'But you're not handling it.'

'What?'

'Running away isn't handling it.'

'Yes, it is. I'm *managing* it. I'm saving my family and friends from it.'

'Well, that's all very well and good for you, but what about the rest of us, the ones who can't run away? If you're so great at handling it, what are your tips for me?'

She stared at him, slightly exhilarated by her outburst. It was as if something had been unlocked, a room full of fury she hadn't known existed.

'Isabella, I didn't mean...'

'No, you didn't mean anything because you didn't think. You did what was best for you, and didn't worry about anyone else.'

'That's not fair. I was thinking of my family, my friends. And yes, I chose them over you. But not because I wanted to. I never wanted to have to make such a decision.'

Yet he had. And with an ease and surgical swiftness that he couldn't have done if he'd really cared for her.

'Your concern about your family sounds noble, but, honestly, I wonder if it's just an excuse.'

'What are you talking about?'

'Your family are really the reason you left?' she asked, knowing the real reason he'd left was because he didn't love her. Because if he had he would have stayed.

Rowan scoffed and stepped back. 'I didn't use

them as an excuse. You saw what happened to them.'

She nodded. She knew what Rowan's family had gone through, but she also knew what sort of intrusions she'd had to endure over the years. She put up with them, others did as well. Why couldn't Rowan?

Because he doesn't love you enough.

These were the fears that usually taunted her in the middle of the night and they were even doing so in London with Rowan standing next to her.

Besides, this wasn't the argument they were meant to be having. There was no way of fixing her broken heart, but they could deal with the problem at hand.

Compartmentalise.

She swallowed down the emotion that was ready to flow over and said, 'I think we do the interview.'

'I think we let the photos be published.'

'I'm hungry.'

'What has that got to do with anything?'

'Nothing, I suppose. Only that maybe it will be easier to decide if we have something to eat. If we can sit somewhere in private.'

She looked around again. London was big. She knew this, logically, but while she could walk across the main city of Monterossa in an hour, London was something else entirely.

'Whose idea was it to go to your hotel?'

'Um, yours?'

'Whose idea was it to walk?'

'Yours again?'

'Yeah, well. I was wrong.'

So wrong. But she hadn't stopped making the wrong decisions all night. This should hardly be a surprise.

A boat with music and a loud party chugged slowly past them.

Tonight was meant to be fun. A celebration! A mood of optimism was in the air in a way it hadn't been for years. But her feet hurt and her stomach growled.

She wondered what Francesca was doing. Hopefully she was already in bed.

Isabella groaned.

No. Francesca wouldn't be asleep. She'd be worried.

Even more reason to get on with this and decide about what to do next.

CHAPTER SEVEN

IT WAS NOW well after midnight, but with the extended opening hours of the bars and pubs, people still wandered the streets. The route he'd navigated for them hadn't been too crowded and he felt as though the face masks had provided some cover, but he was still relieved to see his hotel come into view. Thankfully the area surrounding the steel and glass reception area was mostly deserted. The sight of him dressed as a waiter from the Aston stumbling into the hotel at one a.m. with a princess was not one they wanted anyone to see.

'Here?'

He was staying in an exclusive boutique hotel, in a high rise overlooking the city. So discreet no one would know at a glance what this unassuming lobby led to. Thankfully, the hotel was so exclusive and used to high-profile guests with odd whims that they didn't even blink when he entered in his waiter's uniform, but simply said, 'Mr James.'

'You're not staying. I've just come to get changed and then we can figure out what we're going to do and get you back to your hotel,' he said to Isabella.

'Of course,' she replied, the same strain he was feeling evident in her tone.

Neither of them wanted her to go back to her hotel tonight, even though they both knew she had to.

He steered her to the elevators, grateful he'd kept his phone and all his cards on him when he'd changed into the uniform at the Ashton. He swiped his card and the elevator took them to the fiftieth floor.

'My ears just popped. Did yours?' she said with a smile.

He'd missed her so much. It was easy to forget the happiness and delight she found in simple things when she wasn't around, but now she was here? Her happiness was infectious.

As they entered his room she gasped.

'Wow. Just wow. This beats a stuffy hundred-year-old place in Mayfair any day. Are we higher than the London Eye?'

You should see it in the daytime, he wanted to say, but didn't.

Because then he really wouldn't get her out of here and back to her hotel by morning.

The view from his room was the best in the hotel, northwest over the city. They could see the

London Eye, the Houses of Parliament, the river. Everything. Even the dome of St Paul's could be made out from the bedroom window. Though he didn't tell her that, in case she went to look.

Food. Discussion. Send her home. That would be all.

His suite had several rooms, including a large living space with several comfortable sofas, all arranged to take advantage of the view. There was a kitchen and dining room too, along with a large bedroom and more bathrooms than either of them could use.

Isabella flopped onto one of the sofas and tugged off her shoes, which, while better than the stilettos, seemed flimsy.

She groaned with pleasure as she rubbed her feet. 'Oh, that feels amazing,' she said.

He had to turn away and compose himself at the sound of her satisfaction.

'I'm absolutely famished,' she said, looking up at him with pleading eyes.

He was hungry as well, the snack he'd had before going out now just a distant memory. 'Of course. What do you want?'

He dialled down to Room Service for cheeseburgers and fries for both of them. Chocolate cake for dessert and a bottle of red. She raised an eyebrow when he specified the Californian pinot, but said nothing further.

Isabella shuffled her body around in her dress,

the dress, or more likely her undergarments evidently giving her grief. 'My bra is killing me. I wish I could get changed.'

If Isabella was relaxed and comfortable, she'd be more likely to think rationally about the photos. They hadn't decided what they were going to do about Sir Liam's offer. They'd reached an impasse and he found he was wound tighter than Isabella's underwear.

'The concierge can probably get you some other clothes if you don't want to go home in your dress.'

'Now?'

'They're pretty good.'

'Do you know this from the last time you brought a woman up here?'

He coughed. 'No, I… I once spilt coffee on a shirt I needed for a meeting and they got a new one for me at seven a.m.'

'Oh.'

The question hung out there, though, unasked. Unanswered.

Have you been with anyone since me?

The answer was short and simple: no one.

He didn't want her to ask the question, not because he didn't want to answer it but because he didn't want to feel compelled to ask the complementary question back. Had she found someone else? He didn't want to hear the answer.

He wanted her to be happy, he needed her to

move on, yet the answer would break him, none-theless.

He handed her the phone. 'A man named Dennis is looking after me tonight. Dial one and ask him for a change of clothes. You'll be more comfortable. Even have a bath if you want.'

'What?'

A warm bath had always been Isabella's stress relief of choice, and he'd suggested it without thinking.

'You always used to, that is. When you were stressed. I'm not sure if you still do.'

Why hadn't he just offered her a stiff drink, as he was planning on having? The idea that Isabella might be naked, wet and slippery two rooms away was psychological torture. Not to mention dangerous.

'I might just get changed, if that's okay.'

'Good idea,' Rowan said.

Yes, a far better idea than suggesting she have a bath.

Rowan looked down at himself and realised he was still wearing the wait-staff outfit from the Ashton. He went into the bedroom and took it off. It felt good to get out of it finally and slip on some of his own clothes. A pair of old, soft jeans and a black T-shirt.

While he waited for Isabella and the food he scanned social media for mentions of them. There were several photos of her and Francesca at the coronation. They both looked beautiful, Francesca in a white dress and coat, but it was the photos of Isabella in her sky-blue dress that made his heart clench. The general consensus was that they were two of the best-dressed guests. Apart from that, there were no other mentions.

Thank goodness.

How could she think he was using his family as an excuse? *Why* would she think that? Of course protecting his family was his main concern, that was why he was currently in this hotel room, hidden away from the world.

And now only one room away from Isabella who was probably taking her clothes off at this very moment...

He had to get her home as soon as possible.

The wine was delivered and he poured them both glasses, starting on his own. Shortly afterwards, the bathroom door opened, and Isabella emerged, wrapped in a giant white bathrobe. She'd washed her face and pulled her hair back into a loose bun.

Unintentionally or not, she looked as though she was settling in.

'Ah,' he managed. 'The change of clothes isn't here yet.'

'No problem, this is just fine.'

He passed her a glass of wine but didn't make eye contact.

This was all just a little too cosy for comfort.

His body was starting to relax with the wine. It was nearly two a.m. and nothing good ever happened after two a.m. Everyone knew that.

She found a spot on the sofa, tucked her ankles up under her bottom and sipped her wine. 'This is just what I needed. Thanks.'

Even as he remembered all the reasons why their break-up had been the right decision, the steady, persistent thrum in his chest was still thumping to the tune of *You idiot...you made a mistake*.

No. Breaking up had been exactly the right thing to do. Didn't tonight prove that? If they had stayed together their life would have been spent dodging paparazzi and managing the media. That wasn't what he wanted.

Her words from earlier popped back into his thoughts.

'That's all very well and good for you, but what about the rest of us, the ones who can't run away? If you're so great at handling it, what are your tips for me?'

It was different for her. The machinery of the palace protected her. He seemed to be a lightning rod for attention and she was better off without him. This wasn't the time to reminisce, or even look backwards, they had to figure out what they were going to do next.

He joined her on the sofa. 'What did you specifically say to Sir Liam?'

'Ah, you know.' She waved her hand around in the air.

'No, I don't, that's why I'm asking.'

She gazed out of the window to the horizon and the edge of the city. 'You can see the planes taking off from Heathrow from up here.'

'And I can see procrastination.'

'I asked him if he could see his way clear to not publishing the photos.'

'You just came right out and said that?'

'Not exactly. I think I asked him if he'd ever had his heart broken.'

'Oh.' The guilt hit him afresh.

'And I asked how he'd feel if the world was publishing stories about him being left at the altar when he was struggling to even get out of bed.'

'Isabella, is that true?'

She gave her head a quick shake. 'I figured the dumped princess card was the best one to play so I had to tell him that, didn't I?'

Rowan's chest constricted.

'Could you really not get out of bed?' His voice cracked on the words. He hated that he'd hurt her. He should never have spoken to her in the bar in Geneva. Never got them both into this mess.

'Well, I wasn't back doing official engagements the next day.'

'But not getting out of bed?'

'I don't remember, honestly. It's probably an exaggeration. I'm fine.'

But was she? Or was she holding something back? No, that couldn't be. She'd always been honest with him and she had no reason not to be now.

But she was different, as he'd noticed earlier in the night. More cautious, not as confident. Whereas a year ago her smiles were instantaneous, now they wavered.

You did this.

'I'm sorry.'

'I know you are. Please stop saying that. I'm fine.'

'No, I'm sorry for ever going over to speak to you in Geneva.'

'Don't say that either.'

'Why not? It's true. You'd have been far better off if I'd stayed away. You'd probably be engaged to a duke, or a Hollywood actor. Someone who's far more comfortable with a public life than I am.'

That was the problem all along; Rowan might have made his fortune, he might have a public profile, but at heart he was still just a kid who'd dropped out of school, who couldn't even balance a tray of glasses. Who didn't know what to do at a duke's ball. Or how to cope with media attention.

'I don't regret knowing you and I never have. I'm sorry you're now stuck doing an interview with me.'

He sat, dumbstruck, ignoring the fact that she was clearly set on them doing the interview.

He had hurt her. Despite all her assurances to the contrary, she'd told Sir Liam that she hadn't been able to get out of bed, that she'd been heart-broken.

From the moment he'd come to her to end the relationship, even to earlier in the evening, she'd insisted she understood and that she was fine. But then, when they'd been looking over the Thames, she'd challenged him. Told him he was using his loyalty to his family as an excuse.

Ultimately, though, it didn't matter if she was over him or not, because not only was he not good enough to marry someone like Isabella, he'd also already been the architect of the biggest royal scandal in recent Monterossan memory—a stag night gone wrong and a cancelled wedding. There was no coming back from something like that, no matter who he was.

A knock at the door saved him. Saved *both* of them. Their food had arrived, not just allowing a very needed change of subject but also a well-needed blood-sugar hit. They ate their burgers in silence except for Isabella's gentle moans at the taste of the burger. They were mopping the sauce from their plates with the fries when she said, 'Oh, my goodness, I think that was one of the best burgers I've had in my life.' She took a large sip of wine and fell back in her chair.

He had to agree. Apart from being extremely satisfying, it had successfully shifted the mood between them. But they still needed a solution to their problem.

'Cake?' she asked, spying the desserts still on the tray. Two large pieces of next-level-looking chocolate cake. The thick slices appeared to be moist, covered in a glistening icing, the plates decorated with other chocolates, and a custard cream sat to one side. He could tell before he even tasted a bite that it would be one of the best slices of cake he'd ever tried.

'Not until we decide what to do.'

'You're holding the cake ransom?'

'No, I think I'm holding us ransom. No cake until we are agreed.'

'You know chocolate cake is my favourite food in the world.'

'I do. That's why I ordered it.'

He met her gaze and held it. It was a mistake because she did as well, rising to the challenge. Calling his bluff.

'To hold it over me?' she asked.

'Honestly, I thought I'd convince you just to agree to let the photos go out. I didn't plan on dragging this innocent cake into our negotiations. It's not to blame.'

She gave him a wry smile. 'You thought you'd be able to convince me to let the photos be published?'

'Yes, but not because I think I'm a master ne-gotiator. I just thought you'd be able to see that a photo or two of us together is far preferable to a tell-all interview.'

If the interview had been with him alone, or even them separately, he might have considered it. But together? With him having to watch her give her answers and repeat the lie that she was fine. That she understood why he left. With him sitting there, wondering how much was the truth and how much was the lie.

You want her to be okay, don't you?

The belief that Isabella was not crushed when he ended their relationship had comforted him over the past year. It had been the one thing stopping him getting on a plane and flying across the Atlantic to beg her forgiveness. He had convinced himself that she also knew he wouldn't have made a very good husband for her. But if he'd been wrong, if she'd been hiding her hurt for all this time, then where did that leave them?

Exactly where they were one year ago. The reasons might have changed, but the facts remained: she deserved better than him.

He couldn't bear the thought of either of them being questioned closely on the end of their relationship. The way things stood between them now was for the best; with her in Monterossa getting happily along with her life, and with him in New York, keeping a low profile. It was best for everyone.

'For starters, they'll plan their questions, they'll

ask the most private, most probing things possible,' he said.

'And we will have prepared answers.'

He sighed.

'They'll twist our words, misrepresent them.'

'That's always a possibility, but when you don't
say anything at all, they just make up things to
fill the void,' she said.

'All they can claim is that the pictures show
two single people who used to be engaged talking to one another. It's hardly scandalous.'

'Neither of us want anyone to know we were
there, and you can't go back to the States and skip
your brother's wedding! If we do the interview,
you can still go.'

But Rowan had already resigned himself to
the fact that he would miss his brother's wedding. Coming back to London had been a mistake. One he wouldn't make again. They were all
better off—his mother, father, brother and especially Isabella—if he stayed away.

'That's not going to be possible.'

'Oh, Rowan, don't be like that! Your family
want you there.'

'So they can read defamatory stories about
themselves the next day?'

'It won't be like that.'

He looked at her and let himself study her properly for the first time since she'd come out of
the bathroom. She was sitting back in the dining

chair, twirling the stem of her glass. Her brown hair that had been so perfectly groomed into shiny waves early in the night was now tied back loosely. Her face was clear of make-up, revealing the real Isabella behind the perfect princess mask.

His Isabella. Because this was how he remembered her when he let himself think of her. Dewy, gorgeous. Real.

He looked away quickly when he realised her robe was falling undone, giving him a glimpse of too much reality.

The sooner they made a decision, ate the cake and got her home, the better.

'How can you still trust them to be half decent?' he asked.

'The press? The public?'

'Yes, after all that's happened?'

She shrugged. 'I guess I think very few people are truly bad. Most people are just doing the best they can.'

He turned away. She always had been able to see the best in people, but, like the privilege of her birth, it was something he'd never be able to share with her.

And where did it leave them? Precisely nowhere and disagreeing on what they should do next.

She reached for the cake.

'Woah, woah. What are you doing?'

'Eating the cake.'

'So we're letting the photo out?'

'No.'

'Then we can't have the cake.'

'I thought you were joking.'

'I never joke about chocolate cake,' he said.

She sat and stared at the cake.

He stared at her.

'Tonight has been an unmitigated disaster,' he said.

Isabella opened her mouth to agree but stopped. His comment felt harsh. Yes, things hadn't gone to plan, but was seeing her, spending time with her, an 'unmitigated disaster'?

According to Rowan, yes. According to Rowan, he couldn't get to the other side of world fast enough. To be away from her and done with her for ever.

He doesn't love you. He probably never did.

'It's been unexpected, unusual, but it's also been an adventure.' She tried to hide the hurt from her voice.

Has it been that horrible to see me?

It had been stressful, at times frighteningly so, but there had been moments. Like in the store-room at the Ashton. Watching Rowan get changed and then...

He kissed you.

He had kissed *her*. Not the other way around. Urgent, but tender. Her pulse spiked at the memory.

Why had he kissed her if he didn't care for her? None of it made any sense.

'Some of it was fun,' she continued.

'Oh, come on. We were trapped in small rooms. We set off a fire alarm. We got caught in several compromising situations.'

'Yeah, those were the most fun,' she muttered, her face warming, knowing he probably wouldn't appreciate the joke.

She looked up and saw him twisting his mouth. Trying not to smile.

Ah.

He *had* enjoyed the kiss.

A sensuous, passionate kiss that had sucked the air from her body and left her still reeling.

'It was stressful and awkward and all those things. But it was just what I wanted tonight to be.'

'You wanted to get papped and walk halfway across London?'

'No. I wanted to have an adventure. Yes, I wanted to have it with Francesca, but I wanted to do something out of the ordinary, something unplanned.'

'This was definitely unplanned.'

'I got to ride on a Vespa. I walked along the Thames at night. I danced with Sir Liam Goldsworthy.'

'That was a highlight?'

'Yes. Not because he's a good dancer but because I was brave.'

'Come on, you speak to heaps of people every day. You were trained to speak to strangers.'

'Yes, I was trained to make polite small talk. Tonight I had to negotiate. I had to go off script and ask for something.'

'And that's unusual?'

'You know it is. When we go to events, they're planned to the last detail. People plan what they're going to say to us, and we know what we have to say back. This was...not like that.'

'So a career as a negotiator awaits you?' He grinned, but he'd touched on something sensitive.

She pulled the robe tighter. 'No, not that. But something else.'

'What do you mean?'

'Things are changing. I need to figure out what I'm going to do with my life.'

'What are you talking about?'

Would he understand that when Francesca's role changed hers had to as well? No one said so, and there were no rules about this sort of thing, but it was just something she felt. She couldn't stay still and keep doing what she was doing while her sister took on an even bigger role.

'My father isn't well.'

'I know. Do you want to call him? Check on him?'

'From your hotel room? No, thanks, I don't want him to have a relapse. No, I mean...'

She took a sip of her wine, but it only contained the last drop. Rowan wordlessly filled her glass and his and waited for her to speak.

'I overheard my parents speaking a few weeks ago. They were alluding to something they didn't want to speak to either me or Frannie about. Mum said he shouldn't decide anything until he'd spoken to Francesca. And then said they shouldn't mention anything to me at all.'

'What do you think they were talking about?'

'Abdication, of course.'

'Why?' He pulled his 'you must be mistaken' face.

'Because that's the one thing that affects her and not me. You know how Francesca and I do everything together, how we always have. We went to school together, we work together. We're the twin princesses. But when she's queen...'

'I thought you didn't want to be queen.'

'I don't. That isn't what this is about. But when she's queen, I'll lose her.'

'You—'

She held up her hand. 'I know I won't lose my sister. But I will no longer be a twin princess. I can't be a twin princess on my own.'

'You're going to have to pretend I don't know what you're saying.'

'I know I'll still have a job, I'll still be Princess of Monterossa, but she'll have an entirely different role. She'll sign all the papers. She'll sit at the head of every table. She'll open parliament every year. She will be the one getting crowned.'

'Ah. Is that what you were thinking when we stood outside the abbey?'

Isabella nodded. Then. All day. And most of the time when she hadn't been distracted on this escapade with Rowan.

'We've always done everything together and now everything is about to change. And I...' She stumbled over her words. 'I feel like I'm being left behind.'

There it was. Raw and true. Her deepest fears. She was, after all, the second princess, the spare. It was probably, subconsciously, why she'd pressured Rowan into marriage as well. So she wouldn't be left behind.

'You don't know that's what they were talking about. It could have been anything.'

'Sure, you guess what they were saying. You need to talk to Francesca about what we will have for dinner. But don't talk to Isabella. You need to talk to Frannie about our summer holiday, but there's no need to talk to Isabella.'

'You need to speak to Francesca about her taste in men. But there's no need to talk to Isabella.'

She let her lips twitch into a grin. 'Okay, point taken. But you know how sometimes you just *know* something? And not because you're being paranoid, but because you just *know*.'

He nodded.

She'd *known* he was going to tell her their relationship was over as soon as he'd walked into her room that day.

She'd *known* that something was wrong when her mother had sat both her and Francesca down to tell them about their father.

'Dad has been really sick.'

'I know, but you said he's on the mend.'

'Yes, but he's weaker and this has shaken them both. The cancer spread to his lymph nodes. There's no guarantee of recovery, particularly as he's had so many complications. He might live another five years, even another ten.'

'None of us know how long we have left.'

'No. But my parents have more reason to doubt than others. I think they may want to make the most of the time he has left. And if it were up to me, honestly, I think he should abdicate. I think he should relax. Not work so hard. I want him to stay with us for as long as possible.'

Her eyes filled at the realisation. Something she hadn't been able to articulate before this point. She actually *wanted* her father to abdicate. She wanted him to look after his health!

Even if that meant Francesca would become Queen.

Even if it meant her own life would change.

'I don't know what this means for me. Where it leaves me. I don't know what my job is anymore.'

She wasn't prepared for the emotion that rose

up in her as she said those words aloud for the first time. Seeing her wipe her eyes, Rowan moved to the chair next to her. He picked up her hands and squeezed them.

'Hey, it is all going to be all right.'

She sniffed, tried to fight back the tears, but then Rowan was next to her, comforting her. And when he put his arm around her shoulder what was she supposed to do but snuggle in and let the tears fall? He was warm and smelt of clean clothes and happy memories.

Her father would be okay, but Francesca would be queen.

And she would be…alone.

A solitary princess, a single woman.

And that would be okay, because everyone around her would be happy. Her sister would be happy, her parents would be happy. Rowan would be happy because he was protecting the people he loved.

Yes, she would be alone, and that would be okay because that was how it was all meant to be. She took some deep steadying breaths with her eyes closed. She was finding her centre, reaching contentment.

She was brave. And it would all be okay.

She opened her eyes but two amber eyes, brimming with concern and mere inches away, looked back at her.

He held her shoulders and what choice did she

have but to keep looking at him? To hold his gaze, to give in to the way her body swung towards him?

After everything they'd done tonight this felt the riskiest. But also the most difficult to stop. It wasn't even as if this would be the first kiss they'd shared this evening, but the second. If you were counting. Which she was.

They weren't getting back together—she was silly but not *that* silly—but he was here, and she was here, and it would be a shame not to enjoy the moment. Life was precious and you only lived once. You had to enjoy every moment you were given, suck every drop of joy you could out of it. Tonight, she wanted to be touched. She wanted to feel alive. So she closed her eyes. She wasn't sure who moved the last inch, him or her, but once their lips were touching it didn't matter. Everything stilled.

She wasn't sure who moved their lips first, but once his were slipping against hers her mind went blank. She wasn't sure who opened their mouth first, but it also didn't matter once her tongue was sliding next to his, his fingers sliding through her hair, her fingers reaching for the fabric of his shirt and clutching it in her greedy fists.

Unlike the earlier kiss, this one was less of a surprise. She had time to take everything in, the things that were the same: his taste, the softness of his lips. The things that were different: his aftershave was new…and of course the beard. It was softer than she'd thought it would be, and it heightened all the sensations in her face and around her lips. But his mouth, his tongue felt the same. And most of all his hands were as they always had been, strong and sure and slipping up her neck, into her hair and sending her body and mind reeling.

Her robe fell further undone and she did nothing to stop it. His hand spread over her shoulder and his fingertips scorched her skin like a flame.

She'd missed this. All of this. Everything about it. She'd missed him…

The sweet sound he made when he kissed her, half whimper, half groan. She'd missed the feeling rising up in her belly now, tight, full, urgent. She moved closer to him, needing to feel his hard body against hers. Needing to act on the want building and whirling inside her.

Her robe fell easily undone like a poorly wrapped present. Realising her bare breasts were tumbling out of it, nipples erect and eager, Rowan jumped away from her, as though he'd been scalded.

'Oh, come on, you've seen them before,' she said, trying to hide the disappointment in her voice. She pulled the robe back around her. It was all too good to be true and she should have known that he would pull away eventually.

'That's the problem. I know exactly what I'm missing.'

That remark filled her with more warmth than his last kiss. He wanted her as much as she wanted him. It wasn't just one-sided. He looked pained, his gorgeous face creased with hesitation.

'You don't have to, you know. Miss it.'

'Izzy, seriously.'

'Seriously. In a few hours the world's going to think we made out in a cupboard. What harm can it do?'

'As compelling as that logic is, it isn't right.' He stood.

She jumped off the couch and went to him.

She wanted this memory. She wanted to remember their last time. Know that it was happening and commit every caress to memory.

'We can worry about the consequences tomorrow.'

'It already is tomorrow.' He raked a hand through already mussed hair. She stepped up to him and repeated his action, running her fingers through his hair, holding his face in her hands. How she adored his thick, soft hair. The colour of golden caramel. He didn't stop her, but put his arm around her waist.

'Well, the next day,' she said.

After they figured out what to do about the photo. After she'd gone back to Monterossa.

She stroked his face, explored his new beard.

Studied it closely from all angles. She hadn't thought it would suit him, but it did. It made him look older, more distinguished. Stronger.

'I like it.' She ran a fingertip along his jawline.

'You need to get back,' he croaked.

'Everyone's going to think we did it anyway. So what's the harm?'

'The harm is that it was difficult enough to walk away from you the first time.'

Nothing could possibly be as difficult as that, she thought.

'It doesn't have to mean anything,' she said. 'It could just be rebound sex.'

'Isn't that usually with another person?'

Was it? She honestly didn't know. The only thing her body was screaming right now was that it had been a year since she'd been with anyone. And that had been the man she was standing with now, her nipples straining to be kissed by him, all sense of logic and sense forgotten when she'd walked through the hotel room door.

'I don't think that's a hard and fast rule.'

She had no idea what was what any more. But it didn't matter—the only thing that mattered was the sensation swirling through her. She was with Rowan. His arms were around her waist and his body was pressed against hers, warm, strong and everything. She was burning inside, desperate.

But sex was just sex, wasn't it? She wanted it and, judging by the way his body felt pressed against her, he did too. They didn't have to deny themselves.

Just rebound sex, but with her ex.

Everyone did it.

Didn't they?

Rowan's eyelids dropped, giving her a moment to study him without being watched. Everything about him was tight, his brow creased, his jaw clenched.

She slid her hand up the nape of his smooth neck and into his hair. Her fingertips almost sparked with the tension crackling over him.

'It doesn't mean anything,' she whispered.

'Isabella.' He said her name in a groan and his lips crashed back to hers. All hesitation gone, the last taste of doubt banished.

Her knees buckled and he caught her, but his mouth didn't leave hers, even as he lifted her up high enough for her to wrap her legs around his waist, even as he carried her effortlessly to the next room and the large bed. Her insides cried with delight and relief.

She fell backwards on the bed and he tumbled on top of her. Shifting her hips, he was now properly on top of her, his hand sliding down her side, over her thighs.

His fingers slid over the softest part of her, the sensitive, secret folds between her legs, and pleasure spread from that point through the rest of her. Her blood fizzed. Realising she could climax at any moment and not wanting to miss the main event, she rolled out from underneath him and turned her efforts to him.

She slid her hands up the back of his T-shirt, desperate to feel the muscles she'd glimpsed earlier that evening. She lifted the hem of his shirt and kissed his stomach, moving higher to his nipples. At some point she was aware that he'd slipped the shirt over his head, given her uninterrupted access to his glorious chest. As she flicked her tongue over his nipples she was vaguely aware that his jeans were going the way of the T-shirt.

'Protection?' she asked. 'I'm still on the pill but maybe we should use something.'

He scrambled around for his wallet and the condom it hopefully contained.

He rolled back to her, the foil packet in his shaking hands.

'Hurry, please.' Desperate, clutching at the last of her resolve, ready to break. 'It's been ages. I haven't…' she panted. 'Not since us.'

He groaned and she felt it vibrate through her, not helping her current status in the slightest. 'Me either.'

That was the cold water they both needed. He held the unopened packet in his still quivering hand.

'It's nearly been a year.'

'I wasn't keeping track.'

'I was. Every single day. There were three hundred and forty-seven of them.'

She opened her mouth from the shock of his confession. He hadn't been with anyone else. He did miss her, truly missed her, in the same way she had missed and longed for him. He stroked her cheek with his thumb, considering, contemplating his next move but somehow his thumb slipped into her mouth, still open with surprise. She caught it, wrapped her lips around it. She could have let it go, but when she saw his irises open she clenched it tighter between her lips, slid her tongue around it and, after a gentle suck, she released it.

His mouth quickly found hers again and any thought of protection evaporated. The last twelve months also evaporated like a dream she'd just woken up from. Rowan lay back on the bed and she slid her body over his. He shifted his weight, helped her on top of him and she was home.

The muscles between her legs clenched and contracted with each stroke as every cell in her body jumped to attention. Most of all, his arms held her and his lips whispered to her, even as he covered hers with soft kisses.

She was out of practice and had been ready to lose herself ever since his lips had first brushed hers in the storeroom, but it was still surprising when the wave hit her. He held her for each shock that came after and they fell together. And they kept falling.

CHAPTER EIGHT

ROWAN SAT IN an armchair angled towards one of the many floor-to-ceiling windows in the suite. The sun had long since come up, and he had watched the light in the sky change from black to blue to pink. Now he looked at the sun bounce in bright bursts off the glass of other buildings across the city.

In the next room he heard her stir.

He hadn't slept all night—there had been more chance of him running a marathon in record time. He clutched a mug of coffee, long since gone cold, waiting for Isabella to wake.

He wished he could say he couldn't believe he had slept with Isabella, but the truth was he'd known all along he'd be powerless to stop it from the moment he'd seen her in Twilight.

You could have stopped it. You could have stepped away.

And the earth could turn away from the sun. Not a chance.

It doesn't have to mean anything.

Those were her words. In the heat of the moment he'd taken them as agreement that this was a one-off thing. But this morning, in the bright light of day, would she still think so? Did he?

A startled 'Argh' could be heard from the other room. 'It's nearly eight!'

He steeled himself.

She swept into the room, pulling the robe closed even as she did, not before he had a further glimpse of what he'd already seen too much of last night.

'We slept in!' she cried.

'You slept in. I was awake.'

'And you didn't make the call?'

He shook his head. 'No. I called him.'

She dropped into the nearest chair. 'You did? Rowan. Thank you.'

She said his name in a rush and he felt it through his skin.

'Why?'

'You convinced me it was the best thing to do.'

That was a white lie. Giving the interview was the brave thing to do. It meant doing something active, taking his destiny back into his hands as opposed to leaving it to the pundits on social media.

And if Isabella could be brave, then he could be too. Though the thought of actually giving the interview had his intestines in knots. Guilt was also a powerful motivator, but he didn't want to tell her that. Guilt about leaving her just before the wedding. Guilt about kissing her last night. Guilt about sleeping with her. Guilt he hadn't been stronger when it had really mattered.

'I did? Really?' Her brow creased and she rubbed her eyes, still heavy with sleep.

'It's what you wanted, isn't it?'

'I never wanted this. Any of this. For either of us.'

'I know.'

'You could have let it go. Pretended you missed the deadline.'

He made a face. 'I'd never lie to you. I'd never do that. No, I think— at least, I hope—you're right. We can have more control over the story this way. It's the sensible thing to do.'

The brave *thing*, he thought.

She stared at him, a goofy smile plastered on her face, the sun streaming in on her, still warm from bed, a crease in the side of her face. She'd never looked more beautiful. A lump rose in his throat and he coughed. 'Well, there's some breakfast in the next room. And some coffee.'

'Great.' She didn't move. 'So are we doing the interview today?'

'No. They haven't decided who they'll assign it to and they'll need time to prepare, but they think later in the week. Probably Friday.'

'I can't stay here all week. I need to get back.'

'They suggested they come to Monterossa.'

'But… How would that work? That would mean you would have to come, too.'

The thought didn't exactly appeal to him, but the thought of attracting more attention in London wasn't great either.

'I have meetings in Paris this week for the launch of the app, so it would be reasonably easy to get to you. Of course, you'd have to clear it with your parents.'

She slumped back down in the chair. 'My parents. I'm going to have to tell them, aren't I?'

Despite last night's dash across London being about protecting her parents, there didn't seem a way around it.

'I'm sure it's far better that they hear something from you than from someone else. And far better that the public doesn't know.'

Isabella chewed her lip and he winced, surpassing the urge to go to her and kissing her worry away.

'I'll figure something out. But are *you* sure?'

Now you ask. 'Yes, I'm sure.'

Go back to Monterossa? To the scene of the crime, so to speak? There was nothing he wanted less. Apart from perhaps answering questions about his relationship with Isabella with one of Britain's most notorious tabloids.

Had he been a serial killer in a previous life? How else could he account for the luck he'd had in the past twelve hours?

Isabella leant forward. The robe she was wearing gaped open and he looked out of the window.

Definitely a serial killer.

'Thank you. Truly. Thank you. This will be fine, I promise.'

He wanted to believe her. He wished he could. But it felt as though he'd just...

'And about last night...'

His stomach dropped. 'Last night was crazy, and stressful, and fun, but we both know it was a one-off.'

Because it's clear as anything that I've blown all my chances with you.

His heart was hammering as he waited for her response.

She smiled broadly and jumped up. 'Good, I'm glad we agree.'

He watched her walk into the dining room and pour herself a cup of coffee.

It doesn't have to mean anything.

But what if it had?

Isabella dressed in the pair of blue jeans, white T-shirt and blazer she found in the bathroom. They must have been dropped off while she'd been sleeping. She couldn't believe she'd slept in and missed the deadline.

Of course you slept. Rowan just gave you the best orgasm you've had in over a year. You haven't felt so relaxed or satisfied in months.

With her body as soft as jelly, it was a miracle she'd woken before midday.

Rowan hadn't been kidding; the butler could get anything. The clothes were exactly her size. There was also a pair of white trainers. When she slipped them on she thought of her poor, beautiful red shoes, left behind somewhere near Westminster Abbey. She called her security detail and requested a car to pick her up.

She had no idea what she was going to say to Francesca, but she'd worry about that when she saw her. She sent her sister a short message.

Good morning, I'm on my way back now.

Rowan was looking at his phone when she came out of the bedroom. Whether it was because he was attending to some work or avoiding her, she wasn't sure.

'Thank you for these,' she said, gesturing to her outfit.

He looked up. 'No problem.'

'And thank you, also, for agreeing to do the interview.' It wasn't what he wanted, but she hoped he'd realise it was the best thing to do.

She desperately hoped it *would* turn out to be the best thing to do.

Last night it had seemed like the best course of action, but this morning, with the reality of having to sit down with Rowan to answer questions,

the thought of Rowan coming to Monterossa…
all of it…small doubts were starting to creep in.

'No need to thank me.'

'There is. I know it isn't what you wanted.'

'It's the least I can do.' He spoke to the ground.

'Hang on, did you agree to the interview out
of guilt or do you really think it's the right thing
to do?'

'Can it be both?'

She sighed. 'You don't have to feel guilty. I
know it was a lot. Being with me.'

If she repeated this line enough she might actually believe it. At the very least, everyone else
would believe it and that was the most important
thing. She was a princess, she had to avoid gossip
and scandal of any kind. She wasn't heartbroken.
She wasn't destroyed. She was *fine*.

Rowan put down his phone and walked over
to her. He placed his hands on her upper arms
and for one glorious moment she thought he was
going to pull her into an embrace. Instead, he
looked into her eyes sternly and she felt she was
about to hear a lecture.

'It wasn't too much. I was just not enough.'

'Rowan. Don't say that.'

'It's true. You need to find someone who isn't
such an obvious target for attention.'

'What are you talking about?'

'Me. My background. My family.'

'There's nothing wrong with your family! The

press just go for any angle they can find. It isn't your fault.'

He hung his head. 'Of course it's my fault. I don't have the first clue how to stay out of the papers—as last night's adventure proved.'

She shook her head. 'None of that is because of anything you did.'

'Exactly, it's about what I didn't do. What I *can't* do.'

'Rowan, you can do anything. You're amazing.'

He sighed. 'No, I can't.'

I can't marry you, was what he was saying. And in the end did his reasons matter?

They had come full circle. Just when she was allowing herself to get her hopes up. To think they might have had a breakthrough, that maybe there was a way around this for them, it came back to this.

There would never be a way around this, there was no way he would ever decide to upend his life and his family's for her. She was in the public eye and everyone she loved would be too. And Rowan, for all his gifts, wasn't prepared to handle it. He didn't love her enough.

'I'd better go,' she said. 'I'll see you later.'

See you in Monterossa. My home. Where we shared so many lovely times. Where you proposed to me. Where I thought we were happy. And where you broke my heart.

Maybe just letting the photos out into the world would have been the better plan.

But it was too late for that.

She lifted herself onto her toes and touched her cheek to his. Her effort not to breathe in his scent was futile. It surrounded her. Coffee, mint and the bed they had shared last night.

Alone in the elevator that took her down to the street, she pressed her palms to her face. This was all her fault, this whole mess. The plan to sneak out of the party at the Ashton, the idea to go to the club Rowan was most likely to be at. The decision to speak to him! And then the decision to do the interview. She'd made mistakes at every corner she'd turned.

Everyone was right; there was a reason she'd been born second. Francesca would not have made these mistakes.

A car was waiting outside the lobby, with a very stern-looking Giovanni Gallo standing next to it. He looked exhausted; dark shadows framed his dark eyes.

'Your Highness.'

'I'm sorry for running away last night,' she said. Now she saw the look of disappointment and annoyance on his face she was even more ashamed. 'Is my sister at the hotel?'

'Yes, ma'am.'

'And…'

Is she very angry? Isabella was about to ask, but thought better of it.

She'd find out soon enough.

Too soon, in fact, she thought as the car pulled up outside her hotel in Mayfair a short while later. Francesca was wide-eyed and pacing the room when Isabella entered. It took about two seconds for her expression to change from relief to fury.

'Where have you been? Where on earth were you? Are you safe?'

'Yes, yes, I'm safe. I was…a few places.'

'Where did you spend the night?'

'At a hotel.'

'Not this one!'

Isabella shook her head.

'Who with?'

Isabella drew a deep breath.

'Please don't yell.'

'That means I'm going to.'

'I was with Rowan.'

'Rowan? *The* Rowan? Rowan James who broke your heart? Rowan James who you still cry over!' yelled Francesca.

'Shh!' Isabella said. 'You said you wouldn't yell.'

'I said nothing of the sort. I've been out of my mind. I've been looking everywhere!'

'I'm sorry.'

'Sorry! You're sorry? I found these!' Francesca reached down and lifted up a pair of red stilettos.

Isabella gasped. 'My shoes!'

'So they *are* yours? Bella, think for a moment how you'd feel if you came across a pair of my shoes, abandoned, outside Westminster Abbey. You have no idea the scenarios that went through my mind.'

'I told you I was safe.'

'Yes, in one single voicemail message hours after you disappeared.'

'I didn't mean to worry you, I wanted to fix things before I called you. And I didn't mean for you to find the shoes, I didn't mean to leave them behind.'

'I thought you'd been kidnapped.'

Isabella's knees buckled.

This was all her fault.

Second Princess Syndrome struck again.

'I'm so sorry. About everything. About making you leave the Ashton, about taking you to Twilight. About always messing up. About everything.'

And then she burst into tears.

Rowan wore jeans and an old shirt, matched with sunglasses and a battered baseball cap, for the walk back across London to his Vespa. Even though he wasn't with Isabella, he still took the back streets to avoid people as much as possible. It was broad daylight after all.

He was mildly surprised to see the Vespa exactly where he'd left it. The back of the Ashton looked different in the day, with no guards or trace of a fire alarm.

He cringed.

He studied the door they had sneaked in through and remembered Isabella talking to the guards, smiling, persuading, and his chest felt tight. She had been brave. She *was* brave.

And she was also right—last night had been fun.

For the first time since they'd broken up, he'd felt alive. Yes, it had been stressful and awful and all those things, but he'd been with her. Even though everything had gone wrong, there was no one else he'd rather have had at his side.

He placed his hand on the bike seat, where she'd sat last night, her breasts warm against his back. Then his mind flashed to later, her bare ankles hooked around his, her bare breasts warm against his pounding chest. Both of them sticky with sweat, dizzy, and spent.

She'd agreed that the love-making had been a one-off. A factor of the circumstances. Nothing to worry about. Or stress over. Just one more strange thing in a very strange night.

It doesn't have to mean anything.

He pushed the thoughts away and climbed on the bike, heading for home.

His parents still lived in the flat he'd grown up in. He'd tried to buy them a bigger place but they'd refused. They loved their home and couldn't imagine leaving it.

'Will said you left early last night,' his mother, Heather, said, sitting across the kitchen table from him.

'Yes. I was tired. After the flight.'

His father, Alistair, laughed. 'He also said you happened to run into a certain princess.'

'What else did he tell you?'

'He didn't say much, only that Isabella was there, there was a kerfuffle with a photographer and you both left in a hurry.'

'Yeah, well.'

Alistair and Heather leant forward, waiting. So he told them. How they'd chased the photographer, how they had been offered the chance to prevent the photos being published in return for the interview. He left out most of the colour and detail.

'We agreed to do the interview. I don't want the press getting wind of the fact that I'm in town and that Will and Lucy are getting married this weekend and Isabella doesn't want to embarrass her family.'

'I think you made the right decision. It will give you more control,' his father said, as though he and Isabella had shared notes. 'And it's an opportunity to promote the new app.'

'I doubt they're going to ask about that.' The media didn't care about his app. Or mental health.

If they did, they wouldn't send paparazzi after princesses.

'Maybe not, but tell them anyway. *Use* them.'

Use them? In Rowan's experience he was the one to get used by the press, not the other way around.

'I'm going to do an interview,' his father said.

'You're what?' Rowan mustn't have heard properly.

'I'm going to talk to some people your communications team lined up.'

Rowan's skin broke out with hot prickles. 'They approached you?'

'No, no. I went to them.'

'I don't understand.' Understatement of the day. Why on earth would his father go looking for an interview? Rowan had spent half the night trying to get out of one.

'I want to support you. I want to help promote this new app. I know you do all right without me, but I want to help. Especially with this one.'

Rowan blinked, studied his sixty-five-year-old father. He knew his lined, weathered face so well that sometimes he didn't even really see.

'When I was a teenager I went through a hard time. You know that. I made decisions I regret, but the thing is, it would have been easier if I'd had support. This app that you've come up with, it's a game changer. A *life* saver.'

Rowan shook his head. It made him uncomfortable when people said that sort of thing to him. He came up with the tools, but it was up to the people to use them.

'Apps like this provide more than just exercises, they destigmatise mental illness, they promote discussions about mental health. It would have changed my life. I feel passionate about it.'

Heather picked up Alistair's hand and squeezed it.

'So I approached your communications team and asked how I could help.'

This was all very well and good but the thought of his father putting himself out there like this, feeling as though he had to, made Rowan agitated.

'You should have come to me first.'

'So you could say no?'

'They'll twist your words. They'll bring up your past.'

'That's the whole reason for doing the interview. I want to talk about it. I'm ready to.'

'You can't!'

'Why not?'

'Because...'

Because he wanted to protect his family. Everything he was doing was to protect them, keep them safe, and now his father went and did something like this?

Rowan put his face in his hands. He hadn't slept last night and was running on adrenaline.

His father's words upset him but he couldn't think straight enough to pinpoint exactly why.

'That's what you came to tell us?' asked his mother. 'That you're doing an interview?'

'That and… I've decided it's too risky for me to go to the wedding.'

'No, Rowan! You have to come.'

He shook his head. 'I don't want to ruin their day.'

'You'll ruin their day by not being there!'

'No, they won't miss me. But they will notice a press contingent and they will notice paparazzi and speculation and goodness knows what other mayhem I might bring along with me.'

His parents looked at one another again and he knew they didn't agree with him.

'The photos may not be published but anyone could have seen me and figured out why I'm here. It's not worth it.'

'Have you told Will?'

'I'm going there next.'

'Maybe think about it a few days, wait until all this calms down.'

'No, he'll need to get another best man. Best I tell him sooner rather than later. My relationship ended because of the lies; I don't want theirs to as well.'

'Hm.' Alistair sat back in his chair.

'What?' Rowan asked, knowing he'd regret it.

'You listened to them, didn't you? You believed the headlines.'

'I don't know what you're talking about.' Maybe he would after a proper night's sleep. Maybe he would if he didn't still smell Isabella on his skin.

'I never believed the headlines. Your mother never believed the headlines and I'm sure Isabella didn't either. But you believed them. You took them to heart, didn't you?'

'The photos with the women weren't real.'

'And all the things they said about you not being good enough weren't true either.'

Rowan grunted. That was debatable. Besides, he had turned out to be an unworthy coward, just as they'd said. A dropout. A failure.

'I'll never believe anything published in the papers again after everything with Isabella.'

Alistair shrugged. 'And you should trust everyone else not to as well. We're big kids, Will is too.'

'It's not that.'

'Then what is it again? Why did you really end things with Isabella? Did you not want to marry her?' his mother said. 'If that's the case, then that's fine. But what if it isn't?'

He wanted to groan but kept it in. He'd never wanted to break up with Isabella, he simply wished he'd never got involved with her in the first place.

Which was why he'd had to end things. To protect everyone. Isabella included.

His temples throbbed.

Protect them from what?

Maybe his father was right. Maybe he did think he wasn't good enough.

Preposterous. You're clever. Kind. Successful. Strong.

He'd been strong enough to break off his engagement to protect everyone he loved. He'd been strong enough to stay away from Isabella every day for the past year. He'd ended the relationship to protect his family, to protect Isabella. They were all wrong. He'd done the right thing.

The Saint Francis hospital had carpeted floors and original artwork on the walls but it still smelt like a hospital. Her father was in the largest suite, reserved exclusively for royalty and VIPs, but it didn't matter how luxurious it was, this was still a hospital and the King was as vulnerable as anyone else to disease. Not for the first time, Isabella felt helpless, but also guilty. It was an entirely preventable disease that had brought him here.

She stood at the door and braced herself to see her parents, but her resolve crumbled as soon as she saw their smiling faces turn to her. Her heart dropped and any sentences forming in her head evaporated. They were sitting in the two armchairs next to a window overlooking the hospital gardens and holding one another's hands.

Isabella was almost thirty, yet she didn't want

to disappoint them. Or hurt them in any way, particularly not now. Exhaustion was catching up with her; she'd travelled to London and back in the past forty-eight hours and had barely had eight hours sleep, on top of everything else.

Francesca hadn't let what had happened in London slip to their parents and neither, as far as she was aware, had the bodyguards. They were no doubt worried about what her escapade would mean for them, but everyone had come home safely and Francesca seemed to have smoothed it over with the security detail. For that she would be eternally grateful, though she had no idea how she'd managed it.

As discreet as everyone else had been, Isabella had decided it was best to come clean with her parents about everything. More lies on top of the current mess would only make her feel even sicker about the whole thing than she already did.

Besides, she had to let them know why she was doing an exclusive interview with *The Truth* without going through official palace channels and why Rowan would be stopping by Monterossa for a visit later in the week. That would hardly go unnoticed.

'Darling!' said her mother, 'It's so good to see you. How was London? We saw the photos.'

Isabella's heart stopped.

'Photos?'

'Of the coronation. You both looked beautiful.'

Isabella's heart began beating again, but her fingers still shook from the adrenaline shot resulting from her mother's remark. 'Thanks. How are you both?'

'Very well,' said the King, almost beating his chest. 'They're saying I may be able to go home as early as Tuesday.'

'That's great,' Isabella said but her voice was tight.

Her mother studied her through narrowed eyes and Isabella sat on the edge of the bed.

'What's up, darling?'

Before she could change her mind, Isabella let it all fall out. The crucial points anyway. The kisses and the love-making she kept to herself, but by the end of the rush of information they knew that she had persuaded Francesca to sneak out of the Duke's party, that she'd run into Rowan and agreed to an exclusive interview in exchange for not publishing the photos proving she had left the party.

'I'm so sorry, I didn't mean to let you down. It won't happen again.'

She expected them to say, 'Damn right it won't,' but her father asked, 'Why did you do it?'

'Why?'

'Yes, why?'

'Because…' She couldn't tell them this, could she?

Her father reached out and took her hand in his.

His was pale, cold. And even though it looked like his hand, it was thinner and covered in marks it had never had before.

'Because I'm worried. I thought this might be our last chance to do something like that.'

'Why? What's happening? Is there something wrong with you? With Francesca?'

'No. But there's something wrong with you!'

Her parents exchanged a glance.

'I'm going to be fine, didn't you hear? I'm going home.'

But you're still frail and you won't live for ever and I know you're thinking of abdicating.

Isabella dropped her head. 'I'm worried about you, that's all. It was my fault. I have to take all the blame.'

Her parents exchanged another look. They had always been like this, able to communicate without words. She longed for that kind of connection and it felt like a stab in her gut to know it was unlikely she'd ever find it with anyone.

Anyone other than Rowan.

'I'm the flaky one, and this just proves it,' she said.

'Flaky? What do you mean?'

'You know, I'm the unreliable one. Francesca is the sensible one.'

'What on earth are you talking about?'

'You know exactly what I'm talking about.

She's going to be queen, I'm going to be…well, I'm not sure.'

'But she's going to be queen due to an accident of birth, not because she's better than you.'

'But she is, we all know that. We all see it. She's responsible. I sneak out of parties. She's discreet, well behaved, clever. Charming.' Isabella waved her hand around. 'I make messes. I let the family down.'

Her mother stood and walked over to her, then she wrapped her into an enormous hug.

'I don't even know how to begin to unpack all of that,' the Queen said, pulling away and shaking her head.

'What's to unpack?'

'You don't honestly think of yourself as irresponsible, do you?'

'I try not to be but…'

'Exactly, you try not to be irresponsible, which means you probably aren't. So you made one mistake.'

'More than one. An entire sequence.'

'You made a misjudgement and you tried to fix it. That doesn't mean you're fundamentally irresponsible or unworthy. Everyone makes mistakes.'

It wasn't just one mistake. It was having every single transgression, however small, pointed out to her. And the world at large. The torn dress she'd worn to visit a homeless shelter—

completely unintentionally, but she'd been criticised anyway. Calling the prime minister by the wrong name once—disrespectful, but also unintentional. Being dumped three days before her wedding and having to bear the cost and embarrassment of a cancelled wedding—bad enough if you weren't famous, but excruciating when you were.

The list went on and on.

She couldn't afford to make mistakes.

Isabella knew her sister better than anyone else in the world and even though Francesca could be stubborn and selfless to a fault, she didn't make mistakes. Francesca would be a perfect monarch.

'Darling, did you go to that particular bar on purpose?' her mother asked.

'What do you mean?'

'On the off chance you might run into Rowan?'

'I thought he was in New York. Of course I didn't expect to see him.' But what had made her choose *that* bar? There were thousands of others in London. 'I just went there once before and thought it might be a good place to take Francesca. But I didn't expect to see him.'

'Do you still have feelings for him?'

'Oh, no,' she said but felt her face warm as she spoke. 'I mean, I guess I still care for him.' An understatement if ever there was one. 'But I know he doesn't feel the same way. And I've accepted that.'

It wasn't too much. I was just not enough.

Her mother took her hand. 'You were ready to spend your life with him. It's okay if it still hurts. It's only been a year.'

'Yes, but it's been a whole year! I shouldn't still feel…'

'Feel what?'

Isabella shook her head. She still cared for Rowan but she couldn't still love him. She didn't trust him, for starters. Seeing him was a setback, that was all. By the end of the week he'd be gone again and life would get back to how it was before.

'Nothing, I'm fine. In fact, if this last day has shown anything it's that we could maybe be friends. Really, everything is good.'

She squeezed her mother's hand.

CHAPTER NINE

THEY PUT ROWAN in his old room.

The one immediately across from Isabella's.

It was just for one night, he told himself. His return flight was booked for straight after the interview tomorrow.

Did you really think they would put you in a room on the other side of the palace, far away from Isabella, as though you have been banished?

No, everyone at the palace, the King and Queen especially, had been understanding of his decision to break up with Isabella. No one wanted a royal divorce and everyone knew that the pressure of a very public life was not for everyone. But even so, to be given his old room again. To have to sleep in this bed, where he'd shared so many nights curled up with Isabella, planning their future together...

It wasn't too much. I was just not enough.

He hadn't meant those words. They'd been made off the cuff, without thinking straight. He'd done what he'd done to protect everyone, not because he thought he wasn't good enough. His father had been mistaken.

When the knock at the door came he felt it in his chest. He knew that knock, *her* knock. His body knew her, whether his brain liked it or not.

One more night and then they'd never see one another again.

One more night and you'll never *see her again*, his body whispered.

He opened the door and there she was. Her hair was loose, unstyled, and falling around her face in soft waves. She wore only a little make-up and a navy-blue shirt dress, cinched at her narrow waist with a belt. Chic, but relaxed. Ready for anything. Unlike him.

'Hi,' she said and took a step forward.

He stepped back into his room but still she came forward. She planted a soft, awkward kiss on his cheek, though the awkwardness was all his fault. To make up for it, he leant forward and tried to kiss her cheek, but since she'd already started to move away his lips fell on her nose. Her skin tasted sweet and his head swayed as her scent swirled around him.

He took two steps back.

Ridiculous.

She pressed her lips together, biting back a smile, and closed the door behind her.

'Nervous?' she asked.

'About what?' That awkward greeting? You being in the room across the hall from mine?

'Um, the interview?'

'Yes, I mean, no. I'm trying to stay relaxed.' Trying but failing.

She raised a disbelieving eyebrow but said, 'I expect you're more nervous about the launch next week. Or your brother's wedding.'

Rowan had spoken to Will and Lucy and told them about his decision not to attend the wedding. Will had not accepted Rowan's decision and nor had Lucy.

'I'm not getting another best man, so you'd better come,' Will had told him.

They'd agreed to discuss the matter again after the interview. Rowan knew Will would never forgive him if he didn't attend the wedding, yet would he forgive him if Rowan did go to the wedding and ruined it completely?

He should have been more nervous about the launch of the new app next week, he should have been entirely focused on that. But no. The matter that was taking up all of his grey matter was the one standing in front of him now. And annoyingly, awfully, the thing he was most nervous about was *this* moment. And any other moment where he was alone with her.

Especially like this, in his old room.

'It's just us for dinner tonight. My parents are

spending a few days in Sicily, recuperating. And Francesca's making herself scarce.'

He was selfishly relived he wouldn't have to see any of her family members—those were encounters he really would rather avoid, though the flip side of that was that he had more time alone with Isabella. And that might prove to be just as difficult.

'I hope Francesca isn't doing that on my account. I'd love to see her.'

'No, you wouldn't. She's not happy with you.'

'Me? What did I do?'

'No, you're right. She's more annoyed with me for convincing her to leave an official party and then abandoning her. You just got caught in the blow back.'

'Does she know about the interview and why we're doing it?'

'Yes. I came clean with her and my parents.'

'You told them everything?'

She looked down. Was that colour high on her cheeks?

'Not everything. Just about the photos and the interview.'

It wasn't his business what she'd told them, or even what they thought. The only thing he needed to know was that they were letting them do the interview.

'I'm glad they found out from me and not the papers. They agreed that we made the right decision by doing the interview and not causing further embarrassment to everyone by having the photo get out.'

Rowan bristled. Not for the first time that day he remembered his father's words; Alistair had also thought an interview was the best course of action. Everyone thought doing the interview was preferable to letting the photos out and perhaps they were right. But it was easy for everyone else to say that when they weren't the ones who were going to have to bluff their way through a tell-all interview and convince the world that everything was fine between the two of them.

'We had a good talk. About me. About Francesca,' she said.

'And abdication?'

She shook her head. 'No, we didn't talk about that and I didn't think it was the right time to ask. As much as it hurts me to acknowledge it, it isn't about me. It's between my father and Francesca.'

'It still affects you. It's going to change your life as well.'

'Yes, but not in the same way. Besides, it affects many people, but it is still just something between the two of them.'

He wanted to go to her then, wrap her in his arms and tell her how proud he was of her, how wise she was, but apart from the fear that he'd sound patronising, there was the fear that his gesture would be misinterpreted.

'And we talked about other things as well. They aren't angry with me for leaving the party, at least that's what they say. They say that everyone makes mistakes.'

He shook his head. 'They may be right, but we can't afford to, not when the world is watching.'

She pulled a face and he wasn't sure what she was thinking. Last weekend she'd been as keen as he was to avoid a scandal, now she was saying it was all right to make mistakes? It didn't make any sense.

'So, since it's us just us, I thought we could have dinner out on the terrace and game-plan tomorrow? I think we should think about possible questions, that sort of thing. Our PR team has given me a list of things we should think about.'

'That's a great idea.' Not the 'having dinner alone with Isabella' part but the 'preparing for tomorrow' part.

'See you around seven?'

'Yes, sounds good.'

She turned and stepped to the door and he took the moment to let his muscles relax, but then she turned back.

'And, Rowan. About London.'

'Yes?'

He held his breath. What was he hoping she'd say? That it had been wonderful? That she had no expectations but that she wouldn't mind if it happened again?

'I know it was a mistake. And it won't happen again.'

He nodded, exhaled and felt unexpectedly sad.

Thank goodness it was a lovely evening, not too hot, not too bright. She wanted to be in the open air of the terrace, not inside. And definitely not in one of their private rooms. She'd planned this evening to the last detail. What she would wear, how to do her hair and make-up. What they would eat. She needed to look effortless, nonchalant. And most of all calm. Even though she was in full duck mode—gliding serenely across the surface, but paddling like mad below.

She wasn't exactly sure how Rowan felt about the fact that they had made love in London.

No. Had sex. She had to keep referring to it like that. They had sex. One-off break-up sex.

It didn't mean anything.

And it couldn't happen again. For starters her heart couldn't take it.

The terrace was one of her favourite parts of the palace. It was a sandstone patio overlooking the Adriatic, planted with hydrangeas, lavender and lemon trees. Watching over the whole area was a chestnut tree that was said to be older than the royal family. It was a small comfortable area, used mostly for intimate family occasions. To her it was home. Her back garden.

Rowan had seemed overawed by it the first

time she'd brought him here, but she thought he'd become more comfortable over time. This evening though he stood awkwardly, waiting for her arrival.

He wore tan trousers and a white shirt, no tie, with the top button only undone, and looked as though he'd rather be anywhere else in the world.

A jug of iced water sat on the table, glistening with condensation. She poured them both a glass.

'So,' he said as she passed it to him. 'We need to get our stories straight.'

'Don't we have them straight already?' She knew why he'd left, or thought she did. She'd swallowed his excuse, accepted it at face value. The pressure was too much and he didn't want to expose his family to the spotlight.

'Yes, I mean…' He wouldn't meet her gaze and her body stiffened.

'Rowan, did you lie about why you ended our relationship?'

'No. Of course not. It was because of my family. The pressure they were under.'

She did believe him—she always had trusted him—and she'd also always known that any partner of hers would have to be willing and able to put up with the sustained pressure of public scrutiny. But why would he start this conversation with the comment he had? What story did he need to get straight?

It wasn't too much. I was just not enough.

'You're shifting from foot to foot,' she said.

'So?'

'So, Rowan, what's going on? What aren't you telling me?'

'Nothing. Nothing at all.'

'I don't believe you.' It felt good to say it, to challenge him up front, even if she didn't want to hear the answer. She was being brave.

'If you must know...' He pursed his lips together.

'I must.'

'My father said something that's upset me, I suppose. He said he thought I'd used them as an excuse.'

Nausea rose up through her, rippled through her in unsteadying waves. She'd accused him of the same thing.

'But it's not true,' Rowan said.

Isabella's hands shook. 'Then why would he say such a thing?'

'Because he thought I was scared, I guess.'

'What would you be scared about?' Her voice came out ragged.

What if he hadn't broken up with her because he'd wanted to protect his family? What if the real reason was that he simply hadn't wanted to be with her? That he'd changed his mind about her? It was the fear that woke her in the middle of the night. The one that chased her in her dreams.

He just didn't love you.

'Nothing, that's just the thing. I think he was trying to tell me that it was okay, that he didn't mind the articles about him, that he didn't mind his past being picked over and criticised.'

'And?' But if Rowan's problem had never really been about his family, but something else, about his feelings for her, then it didn't matter what his father said. She held her breath and her heart held its beat waiting for his answer.

'It doesn't change anything. They might think they are happy to be tabloid fodder but I'm not happy for them to be so.'

'You're still hiding behind them, then?'

'What's that supposed to mean?'

Indeed. What was it supposed to mean? What did she want him to say? That he'd used his parents as an excuse because he hadn't loved her enough to marry her?

Or that he'd made a thoughtless mistake and that he wanted her back?

She shook her head.

Yes. That. There was still a part of her that wanted him to say that.

Of course, it was a perverse kind of hope, because even if he did say that she couldn't seriously say yes.

He dumped you! Humiliated you in front of the world!

She couldn't get back with him. It was a ridiculous idea.

'We're going to have linguine with clams for dinner.'

He smiled. It was his favourite.

'So, should we start going through this list from the communications team?'

'Yes.'

They sat on the sofa in the shade of the ancient chestnut tree and faced the ocean. The sun was setting behind them, out of their eyes but lighting up the sky in gorgeous pinks and oranges.

She took out the papers the communications team had given her as well as a notebook and pen so she could jot down ideas for answers. Rowan spied them.

'It's okay for you, your memory is freakish. Some of us need help,' she said.

He shook his head. 'It's not that. Are you nervous?'

She shrugged. 'Maybe a little. I don't do this sort of thing often. And it was my idea, so I'll feel responsible if it goes wrong.'

But the main reason I'm nervous is because you'll be sitting right next to me as I have to answer questions about us. About why and how our relationship ended. And questions about how I feel about it. All while holding myself together. And sounding like I'm honestly okay with it.

'It won't go wrong.' His voice was soft but it

didn't reassure. It simply made her pulse spike. 'We can answer these questions. What have you got?'

'The first is, how did you meet? Easy.'

And it was. He repeated the story about how he'd been in Geneva for a Word Health Organisation mental health convention, how she'd wandered into the bar and they'd begun talking. How he hadn't known who she was to start with.

'They love that part of the story,' she said.

'They do.'

The story was always spun as Rowan hadn't known he'd fallen in love with a princess, but what no one really knew was that she hadn't known who he was either. She hadn't known about his work, or his wealth. They had just met as two people in a bar who'd struck up a conversation about the band that had been playing in the bar.

They watched the sky darken and reminisced about the early days of their relationship, their whirlwind courtship. She laughed more than she had in months. When the sun set they lit candles. The food arrived and they shared a bottle of wine. The questions were easy, straightforward. Factual. They didn't have secrets from one another so it was easy just to give an honest answer. There were questions about their childhoods, quite a few about his career. The usual predictable ones about how she felt about being the second twin.

Whether she envied Francesca. She'd answered that question so many times she could recite the answer in her sleep.

Of course not. I love my sister and she will make a far better queen than I ever could.

Every word the absolute truth.

By the time they had finished eating and drained the bottle of wine she was feeling relaxed and confident. This was a good idea—she'd known it from the beginning.

'Next question.' She read it to herself and said, 'Oh.'

'What is it?'

'Tell us how he proposed.'

'Oh. But that's okay. Isn't it?'

It was. It was a story she'd told many times, only she hadn't told it since the break-up.

'I'll answer that one,' he said.

'No, if they ask me, I have to answer. Besides, it's not as though it isn't on the public record already anyway.'

Her body prickled with awareness and memory. 'Right here, at sunset. You got down on one knee and gave me the ring.'

He nodded. It was the story they had told the world and technically when the proposal had become official, but there was another, far more meaningful moment earlier than that. One that only two people in the world knew about.

He had been heading back to London after a quick visit and she had still been in bed.

'I don't want you to go,' she'd said.

'I don't want to go either,' he'd replied.

'Stay.'

'I have to get back.'

She still remembered how his words had stopped her heart. She'd thought she knew what he meant.

'Stay. Marry me.'

They had stared at one another then, in silence, wondering, waiting. His next words could be life changing.

'Are you asking me to marry you?' he'd said.

She'd nodded.

He'd looked away and the bottom had dropped out of her world. But then he'd turned back and said, 'I suppose there are things to think about, protocols and such, but yes. If you're sure?'

She'd nodded, unable to speak, tears welling in her eyes, and he'd climbed back onto the bed and pressed his soft lips to hers.

Now, Isabella looked out at the dark sea and remembered afresh: *she* had asked him. She'd pressured him into it. That was why he'd left. Because he hadn't meant to propose to her at all. Because she'd pushed him into it too soon.

'I'm not going to tell them the truth. It's too late for that and would sound weird,' she said.

He nodded. 'Yes, it would be strange to tell them that story now.'

She stood and walked to the edge of the terrace and the low stone wall. Looked at the ocean that was now black and invisible.

'Rowan.' She spoke into the darkness. 'If I hadn't asked first, would you still have asked me to marry you?'

'Of course I would have.'

'But were you going to?'

'Yes.'

'When?'

'I don't know. I hadn't set a date.'

'So, you weren't going to.'

'I wanted to marry you. I *wanted* to spend my life with you.'

'But you didn't know when you were going to ask me.'

'No. Isabella, I don't understand what you want to hear.'

She shook her head. She already knew everything she needed to know.

He reached for her hand but she turned her body away.

'Isabella, I loved you. I wanted to marry you. It wasn't easy figuring out how to propose to a princess. But once you asked me, it was easier.'

She went back to the sofa they had sat on earlier, and where the jug of water was. She poured herself another glass for her parched mouth. The water was warm now, but it gave her something to do with her hands.

He joined her.

'I'm not sure why you're asking me about this,' he said.

He was right. There was no point. There was no need to dig up these things. No need to dredge over this history, of all things. No one was going to ask them about her proposal and it didn't matter what his answer was. It didn't change anything and, most of all, it couldn't change anything into the future either.

You were the brave one. And look where it got you.

'No point. You're right. I don't know what I'm saying. Let's get back to the list. The final question.' Her throat was still dry, her body suddenly spent. 'They say we should be prepared to answer a question along the lines of how did you feel about the break-up?'

He looked down.

She knew he felt guilty but it didn't make her feel any better about the situation. If anything, it only made her like him more. None of this was his fault. She could only blame herself.

Just one more mistake to add to the growing list.

'I'm going to say that I was heartbroken, but that I understood your decision and that ultimately it was a decision we made together.'

'That's very kind of you.'

'And I'll say we continue to be good friends.'

'That's also very kind.'

'But it's true, isn't it?' she asked.

Her gaze snagged in his and he held it there. They hadn't seen one another all year because it was for the best, but now they had been thrust together, maybe they could forge a friendship.

He picked up her hand and even as she knew it was risky, this time she was powerless to pull hers away. 'I thought you thought it was for the best if we didn't see one another. I think I thought it would be easier too,' he said.

'And maybe it was what we needed at the time. But now… I don't know.'

'Are you saying you think we can be friends?'

'Yes, no, maybe. I don't know. What do you think?'

'I think…' He continued to watch her as his words trailed away.

Her throat became tight, then the muscles in her chest clenched, the tightness gradually spreading through her body as she sat, still and immobilised under his golden eyes, until he closed them and moved his face towards hers.

She closed her own eyes and fell into the kiss as though she were stepping off a cliff without checking to see how far she had to fall. Without even caring.

She surrendered herself to his lips. And the

consequences. This entire evening had been confusing but this kiss was so simple. The easiest, most natural thing in the world. The absolute only thing in the world she wanted ever again.

Luckily he caught her, kissed her back, pulled her closer. His lips told her a clearer truth; no matter what he might say to her, this was the only story she wanted to hear. The only one that mattered.

He slid his hand up her skirt. Her underwear was thin, practically a formality, and his practised fingers found her soft folds and all the sensitive parts they contained. The desire grew up inside her, the tightness rising to its ultimate climax. He continued to kiss her as his fingers rubbed and stroked and the stars spun in the sky above her like a planetarium. Thinking of the stars, she looked down at herself, at him, his hand up her skirt, her heart exposed.

What are you doing?

Isabella pushed him off her. He moved easily but it was still the heaviest weight she'd ever had to move. She couldn't do this with him. Not again. Not now. Not here.

'I think that being friends with you is risky,' she panted. 'I'm not sure if we have the same definition of friendship.'

'I… I'm sorry. I didn't mean… I got carried away.'

She straightened herself up. 'I let myself get carried away.'

'No. I...'

'What are we doing here, Rowan? What's going on? Once is a mistake, twice seems deliberate.'

'I thought you said mistakes were okay.'

'I meant *public* mistakes.'

Not the kind of mistake where I put my heart and body on the line and you stomp on them.

'I don't know what is going on. I don't know why we can't seem to keep our hands off one another,' he said.

'Could it be that we're not over one another?' It could be as simple as that. Or as complicated.

'Maybe, but, Isabella, you know as well as I do we can't go back.'

She nodded.

Of course they couldn't go back, but could they go forward? Could they start again? Would things be different this time around? No. Because he didn't love her. At least, not enough.

'And you said you understood that we just weren't meant to be,' he said.

Had she said that? She could hardly be expected to remember everything she'd ever said. Or have to hold to everything she'd said to fool herself. And fool him that everything was okay.

Because suddenly it just wasn't.

'I wouldn't quite put it like that.'

He shrugged. 'But you seem happy.'

She blinked. 'Of course I seem happy. I'm putting every ounce of energy and effort I have into seeming happy.'

'So, you're not? Happy?'

Something snapped. They were no longer rehearsing the interview. She didn't have to pretend. She didn't have to put on a brave face.

'No! I'm not happy. I'm angry and hurt and embarrassed!'

The dam was cracked and soon it was fully breached. Everything came out. 'You dumped me three days before our wedding! And that would be bad enough except that everyone in the world knew! No one calls off a royal wedding just before it's about to happen! Never! My name is never printed anywhere without being preceded by the word "jilted".'

Rowan's mouth was open, jaw flapping in the breeze. She didn't care and she couldn't have stopped herself if she'd wanted to.

'*"Jilted Princess Isabella and her sister Francesca attended the coronation." "Princess Francesca and her jilted sister, Isabella, were seen visiting their father in hospital."* Every. Single. Time. It's okay for you, your name is always preceded by "billionaire" or "tech genius" or even "entrepreneur". You are never, ever, *"Love Rat Rowan James"* or *"Princess-Dumper Rowan James".* Yet you tell me that you're the one being treated poorly by the press.'

Rowan looked down and she caught her breath, shaking with adrenaline.

'Are you finished?'

'I'm barely started. I might be understanding, but I'm still hurting. I'm still angry. I'm still upset.'

'Oh.'

'You broke my heart. I might understand why you did, but that doesn't make my heart full and healed.' Her heart would never be complete again.

She'd been trying so hard, so, so long to stay cool. To give the impression that everything was fine. That she understood. Not to make a scene. But it wasn't fine.

She wasn't fine.

She hurt. While logically she knew why he'd done it, her heart did not.

'What more could I have done?' he asked.

'You could have fought for me. You could have tried. You could have been stronger.'

His face was nearly as red as his beard. 'Isabella, I tried. But I couldn't do it. I couldn't make it work. Maybe I wasn't good enough to fix it.'

'You keep saying that, but I don't believe you for one second. You are amazing. You were always enough. There was nothing you had to fix. The truth is you just didn't love me enough. So how about we start calling it what it was? You didn't love me.'

'Isabella.'

This was his chance to deny what she'd just said. To explain.

To say something.

It was strange that a simple flick of the eyes could break your heart, could pry your heart open and crush it. And the look he gave her just then did exactly that.

'We have to be over. I can't do this. We can't go back,' he said.

'No. We can't.'

With shaky knees she stood and walked away as quickly as she could.

CHAPTER TEN

RICHARD WEBBER, THE JOURNALIST from *The Truth*, arrived promptly at the palace, with a photographer in tow. Both men were shown into the reception area where Rowan and Isabella were waiting. The Blue Room was a large airy room with cool stone floors and a view of the ocean. Its walls were lined with artwork by the old masters. It was a room the family only used for official business, designed, he supposed, to give the family a home court advantage.

Which suited Isabella, but Rowan felt as much a guest in this room as Webber.

Rowan hadn't spoken to Isabella since she'd stormed off the terrace last night, leaving him shaken and reeling. Paralysed with guilt. He'd kissed her, begun to make love to her and then tried to tell her it was just a mistake. And she'd rightly given him a dressing-down. And not just about the kissing and making love when he had no intention of taking things further, but also for his behaviour last year.

She was right; he was a coward.

Always would be.

He'd stuffed up.

He'd gone to her room later last night, when he had judged that she might have cooled down, but she hadn't answered his knock.

And his cowardly self was glad because he didn't know what he could possibly say to her to make it up to her. All this time he'd been deceiving himself with the thought that she understood why he'd had to leave and told himself that made it all okay.

But even though she had understood, she still hurt. She was still angry. He'd been fooling himself, telling himself that she wasn't heartbroken, that she didn't love him. But that had just been a story, a way of softening the scandal. It was easier to swallow than the truth.

The air zapped between them while they waited for Richard. Isabella was wearing a white shirt and a full linen skirt that accentuated her waist and gave her a classic elegant silhouette. Her hair was tied back neatly. She looked sharp, sophisticated and utterly untouchable.

After the interview they would each have some photos taken, but not together. They had specified that in the fine print of the contract; even though they were giving a joint interview they did not want a visual image suggesting they were back together going out into the world.

Especially not after last night.

He'd hurt her. More than he'd thought.

No, you hurt her more than you let yourself believe.

She was right, he'd hidden behind some sort of moral prerogative to protect his family, but really he'd been a coward.

The truth gnawed at him, sickened him.

He watched her now. She stood at a window, looking out onto the garden and, beyond it, the sea. She had been polite this morning. But the politeness was damning and perfunctory. He was counting the minutes until the interview would be done and he could leave Monterossa.

Yes, run away, like the coward you are.

He bristled at his inner voice. But what other choice did he have but to leave? She hated him. There was nothing to stay here for.

You fool. She loves you! Still.

That was what her outburst last night was all about. If she didn't have feelings for him would she be that mad? She'd been hiding her feelings about the break-up because she thought that was the sensible thing to do. She'd been taught all her life not to make a scene. To be calm. Composed. *And that's what she did with you when you called off the wedding. But it's all been a lie.* She was hurt and wasn't at all fine. Leaving Monterossa wouldn't fix it.

What could he do to fix it?

Tell her how you really feel. Tell her you were terrified of marrying a princess.

He shook his head. That wouldn't help anyone one bit. And it wasn't true. He'd be stacking lies on half-truths. Rowan was wrestling with these thoughts when the journalist was finally shown into the room.

Isabella's demeanour changed instantly from frosty to warm. An act for Richard Webber's benefit. Rowan tried to muster up some fake warmth of his own.

Webber seemed nice, friendly. A little bumbling even. Rowan didn't feel intimidated by him one bit.

It's an act. Just like the one you and Isabella are putting on. He's trying to appear unassuming, to put you at ease so you think you are friends and so you spill your guts to him.

After they exchanged greetings and pleasantries, Richard said, 'I must say I was surprised to hear that you had agreed to do this interview together. And that you approached *The Truth*.'

'Sir Liam is a friend of mine,' Isabella said smoothly and sincerely.

'But why now?'

So the journalist didn't know about the photos in London. Or if he did, he was going to wait for one of them to say something first.

'Enough time has passed, I guess. And we

wanted to set the record straight. It felt like the right time.'

'Very well.'

Richard started by turning his attention to Isabella and made the usual enquiries. Questions Isabella could answer in her sleep.

'It can't be easy being number two?'

'How was it growing up next to Francesca knowing she would one day be queen but you wouldn't?'

'The second in line to a throne is usually the naughty one. What was the worst thing you did as a child?'

'Didn't you ever want to rebel?'

She'd been answering these questions all her life. She had this.

Rowan realised he was watching her closely as she gave these answers and pulled himself back.

'Are you ever jealous of your sister?' Richard asked.

Isabella smiled but the side of her mouth hardened, in a way he hadn't noticed before. It was probably because he rarely saw her side-on. The sensitive skin at the corner of her lips looked brittle.

She was hurt. The questions were hurting her. How had he not seen that before? She might be smiling and giving well-practised answers but each time she did, she ached.

'Not at all. If anything, she's jealous of me.' Isabella smiled broadly and her eyes twinkled, but to one side, he could see the muscles in her neck tighten against her delicate skin. At that moment he wanted to reach over and strangle Webber, but he kept his own hands clenched in his lap.

'How did you feel when Rowan left you days before the wedding?'

She gave the answer she'd rehearsed the previous evening. Calmly, even smiling. 'It broke my heart, but I understand why he had to do it. It isn't easy being royal, it isn't easy being in the public eye and, honestly, how could I wish that on someone I care about? It wouldn't be fair.'

It broke his heart.

That was the answer she'd always given, and it was what she'd told him when he'd ended their engagement. But he knew now that it was a lie. It was what she felt she had to say, to keep the peace, to avoid upset. To avoid making a scene. But inside she was truly hurt—and still hurting.

It was bad enough he'd done that to her, but now she was forced to keep reliving it—while smiling!

Rowan wanted to push his face into his hands and howl but he kept a sad, contrite look on his face.

This was how she felt all the time. Smiling while her heart was breaking.

Rowan was so busy reeling from these revelations he didn't notice at first when Richard turned his attention to him, which meant he was on the back foot from the outset.

'Tell us about your childhood.'

'It was a normal, happy childhood. I lived with my parents and my brother. They worked hard, loved us both. Gave us all the opportunities they could. My parents are dedicated workers who have helped people all their lives. My brother, too. He's a nurse. I'm in awe of how they have all dedicated their lives to helping other people.'

The edges of Webber's eyes twitched. 'Doesn't your app do that too?'

'Yes, of course. I only meant it takes a very special person to care for and directly support people in need.'

'Of course, we know about your brother, Will, who was with you at your infamous stag night.'

'Those photos were taken out of context. The newspaper sent the women there.'

'Of course, of course,' said Webber. 'I just meant we know that he has had some relationship troubles since that night.'

Rowan had had to end his relationship with Isabella because of press intrusion, so to have this man question him about this now was causing every muscle in his body to knot. His jaw was hardly open as he said, 'My brother and his fiancée are very happy and I do not wish to breach their privacy any more than it already has been.'

Isabella sucked in a deep breath. Rowan turned

and saw that she was smiling warmly and nodding. 'It's okay. Keep going,' her expression said.

Rowan felt as if the interview was already heading off track. He hated answering questions about his family and he sensed that he had said something wrong but wasn't sure what it was. All he knew was that he was furious; if it hadn't been for the likes of Webber and the paper he worked for, he and Isabella might still be together. If only there were a future where tabloids didn't exist, a future where social media didn't exist.

'Tell us how you came up with the idea for MindER.'

He exhaled. This was easier, he was on much safer ground. It was a story he'd told many times. About his father's smoking habit, about how he had come up with the idea at just the right time. How supporting people's mental health was his passion. He almost began to feel comfortable again.

'The app uses many of the same techniques that other apps do. We offer guided meditations, breathing exercises, but also self-guided cognitive behavioural therapy.'

'And what is that?' Webber asked.

'It is a type of therapy that involves breaking down your thoughts, feelings and beliefs and challenging negative thoughts. While we can't change what is happening to us, sometimes we can change the way we think about it.'

'You can't change the world, but you can change what you think about it,' Webber clarified.

'Yes. We're launching a new feature for teens next week and hope people find it as easy to use and as helpful as the other applications we have. Teenage mental health is a difficult area and I'm looking forward to seeing what people think and then continuing to make these apps as good as they can be. But I do always want to stress that while our apps can help, that cannot replace the advice of a fully qualified professional and they are designed to be used in conjunction with other treatment plans.'

It seemed like only moments later that Webber turned his questions back to Isabella.

'How's your father?'

'He's doing much better. He had us worried for a while but he's out of hospital now, which is a big relief to us all.'

'We're all glad to hear that, but do you think he will remain king for much longer?'

'Hey,' Rowan said. That was none of Webber's business. As Isabella had said, that was between Francesca and her father.

'That wasn't one for you, Mr James.'

'No, but is it one for her?'

She touched his knee. Rather than having the calming effect she intended, it made his heart rate spike.

'It's okay,' she said. Turning to Webber, she

continued, 'My father is making a good recovery and we have every reason to think that he will be with us for a long while yet.'

'How do you feel about the fact that your twin sister will shortly be queen? What will you do with yourself then?'

'As I said, my father is going to be with us for many years yet and I will be delighted for Francesca when she becomes our queen. She will be a wonderful monarch and I look forward to doing what I've always done: supporting my family in any way I can.'

Webber smiled. He almost seemed sincere. 'Thank you, I think we're nearly done,' he said.

Relief rose up like a giant bubble in Rowan, instantly making him feel lighter.

They had done it! There had been a few hiccoughs but, overall, it had gone well. He turned to Isabella, who was looking serenely ahead, and he couldn't help but smile. As he always thought when he saw her, she was the most beautiful woman he'd ever laid eyes on.

'I just have one more question. In the future, do you ever see yourselves getting back together?'

Unlike the other questions, this one wasn't directed to just one of them. Who should take it? They looked at one another, and at the same instant she shook her head and said, 'No,' he said, 'The future?'

Webber stifled a snigger. 'Does that mean you are back together?'

Rowan looked sideways at Isabella, hoping for assistance, but she was red-faced and wide-eyed.

'No. We're not. Definitely not. I mean, I just meant…' Rowan stumbled over his words. 'It was the way you phrased it. The future is a long time.'

'And what, exactly, does that mean?' Webber asked.

Rowan couldn't explain because he had no idea himself.

'Of course, what I meant to say…'

Two sets of eyes looked on eagerly.

'We're friends, clearly, otherwise we wouldn't be doing this interview together. And circumstances, such as they are, are not…that is… There were good reasons we broke up and those reasons remain. But we are good friends.'

Webber stood. 'Have you considered a career in politics?'

Rowan, shocked, shook his head.

'Good, because you'd have to be far better at answering questions than that.'

'Hey, I just…you're not going to put that in the article, are you?'

Webber nodded. 'I doubt my editor would publish it.'

That wasn't the reassuring answer Rowan was looking for.

'Richard, would you like a tour of the palace

before you leave?' Isabella asked. Webber's eyes sparkled.

'I'd love that, thank you.'

Isabella waved Rowan back down dismissively. 'No need for you to come.'

Webber looked from him to Isabella and back again and said to the photographer Rowan had completely forgotten about, 'Why don't you take Mr James's shots now, Thommy?'

Isabella and Webber stepped out and Rowan stood to face the photographer. He tried to smile and pose as best he could but he kept wondering what on earth Isabella and Webber were talking about.

'You have to relax, mate. I'm sure she can handle herself,' Thommy said.

Rowan glared at the man. If he was ambivalent towards photographers before, now he positively loathed them.

Isabella showed Richard Webber out of the door and into the rest of the reception areas of the palace. As the Palace of Monterossa was the main residence of her family most of the year round it was not open to the public. Visitors, though, did appreciate tours of select public reception areas and Isabella led him through them now. He smiled and murmured appreciatively as she pointed out the artwork, the furnishings and the sculptures the di Marzanos had collected over the years. He would hardly notice the favour she had to ask him.

'It's funny, you know, how people get nervous in interviews.'

'Were you nervous, Your Highness?'

'No, not me. But I think Mr James was.'

'Why would he be nervous? He's a successful businessman, entrepreneur. He speaks publicly all the time.'

Indeed, thought Isabella. Why on earth would someone as successful and accomplished as Rowan ever be nervous? About interviews? Or marrying princesses? Or marrying the woman he professed to love?

No. He wasn't insecure about marrying her, he simply didn't love her enough. Even though he'd broken her heart, she had to defend him. Both their reputations depended on it.

'The scrutiny a member of a royal family receives is intense. It is hard to understand how intense until it happens to you. He might be comfortable when he's working, but giving an interview with your ex, who just happens to be a princess, is a completely different thing.'

'What are you trying to say?'

'Only that he just stumbled over that question because he thinks it will hurt me less not to deny it. He didn't mean it. We're not getting back together. He just said that to protect me.'

Because after everything that had happened, he still thought of others first.

'But would you?'

She looked around, to look anywhere but Richard Webber's face. She caught her reflection in one of the many mirrors nearby. Just as she thought. Bright red.

'Don't be ridiculous, the man practically left me at the altar. Of course we don't have a future together.'

Webber gave a non-committal shrug.

'So to print that we might would just be cruel. And untrue.'

'I understood this was to be a tell-all interview. No topics off-limits.'

Why was she bringing even more attention to what had just been an awkward stumble?

Because it wasn't nothing.

It was important to you.

When he'd said, 'The future?' the crack of hope she'd been trying to clasp tightly shut had begun to pull open again.

'Yes, you're right. I'm sorry. I was only trying to protect him.'

'We're off the record now, Your Highness. So tell me, why would you want to protect him after what he did?'

Isabella knew there was no such thing as off the record. A principle her parents had instilled in her from an early age.

'Because it's the decent thing to do.'

He raised an eyebrow.

'It seems to me that…things might be more complicated than you are saying.'

'Things are always complicated, but trust me when I say that Mr James and I will never get back together. Now, I think Mr James will be done with his photos. I imagine it's my turn.'

Richard Webber just nodded and followed her out of the room.

Isabella knew she should smile and continue the friendly banter, but her heart was in her throat, stifling her vocal cords.

Rowan had left the room when she returned to have her own photographs taken. Isabella suggested they go outside into one of the palace courtyards; she wanted to distinguish her photos from Rowan's. She did not want to do anything to make it look as though they were back together.

They were not getting back together. If that wasn't already obvious to her, he'd told her as much the night before. Their one night in London had been a blip only. A setback. It hadn't been the beginning of a new future as she'd let herself believe for a few unexpected moments last weekend. They were over. Finished. And there was no path around that. If she let herself wonder about that for even a moment she would fall down a dangerous rabbit hole of hope, fantasy and ultimately pain.

Except…

The future is a long time.

Isabella smiled, looked calm. Smiled again. She had done so many photo sessions in her time she could teach models how to do it. Push your chin forward, tilt your head. Breathe out, small smile, big smile. Repeat.

It wasn't long before she simply said to the photographer, 'I think you should have everything you need.' She didn't wait for him to object and returned directly to the Blue Room.

Rowan was standing there, suitcase at his heels.

Isabella inhaled. This was it.

Goodbye.

For ever.

Except…even as she knew she should simply turn and leave, she had to ask. '"The future is a long time?" Rowan, what was that about?'

Rowan shrugged, studied the Botticelli hanging on the wall. 'I don't know. Maybe it was the way he phrased the question.'

I managed to answer it, she thought with gritted teeth.

It wasn't just last Saturday. Last night he'd had his hand up her skirt, she'd been seconds away from ripping his shirt off.

'What did last Saturday mean to you? What

did last night mean? Really. I know I said it didn't mean anything, but why did it keep happening?'

He grimaced, as well he might. 'Isabella, when it comes to you, I'm powerless. I still care for you. I've never made a secret of that. But you know we wouldn't work.'

She nodded and looked away.

'I'm not sure why you're so upset. It's not as though you would take me back,' he said.

Would you? Would you take him back?

She'd be a fool. Worse than a fool, she'd be… she'd hurt her family, her country. She'd look like a chump.

'Are you asking?'

'I…no. I was being rhetorical. I expected you to say, *Of course not.*'

Of course he wasn't asking. Which was just as well because of course her answer would be no.

A hard, definitive no.

He tilted his head.

She shook hers.

'No. We don't have a future.'

The future is a long time.

What if…what if the world changed? What then? What if *he* changed?

Rowan stepped up to her. 'Isabella,' he began, and her insides melted. Every time he touched her, Isabella's defences disintegrated. It couldn't go on. She couldn't go on like this. She needed a clean break.

This had to be over. And now.

'It's time for you to leave. But before you go, I want to make one thing very clear.' She was going to be brave. She could do this. 'We will never get back together. Not now and not at some time in some theoretical future. I need someone who will stick by me no matter what. I need someone who can be strong for me when I can't be. I need someone who can handle the circus of the palace. I deserve someone who is all those things. That person may not exist and that is fine. But I can't keep doing this. I can't keep pretending I am fine. I can't keep lying.'

A noise behind her made Isabella turn her head.

Richard Webber and the photographer were standing in the doorway.

Perfect.

Of course they were.

Of course nothing would ever go smoothly, nothing would ever go as planned.

This was life. You couldn't change everything, you couldn't fix everything, and you couldn't hide everything.

Isabella nodded to them and turned back to Rowan. She was sick of pretending, sick of being calm. And tired, so tired.

'You hurt me. You didn't just break my heart, you crushed it. You crushed *me*.'

'Isabella, we're not alone,' he hissed.

'I know. And I don't care anymore. I'm so tired of pretending.'

'Izzy…'

His nickname for her hardened her.

'No. There is no Izzy. And I need to set this straight.' She glanced over her shoulder back at the journalists to be sure they could hear.

'I need someone who can be strong. And yes, I know being with me isn't always easy, but do you know what, Rowan? No relationship ever is. Every long-lasting relationship is hard. Every relationship will have ups and downs and you are going to face something far worse in the future than an intrusion of privacy. Someone you love inevitably will get sick, people will leave you. And those are the things you have to be able to get past. Not some silly photographs.'

He looked down. As well he might. She knew she should stop, but she also knew that, like life, things were now out of her control. So she let go.

'I see now you're not the person for me. You're not strong enough, or brave enough. You can't help the person you are and I have no desire to change you. So it's over.'

He looked up and straight into her eyes, his whisky eyes light, his skin pale.

'Really over. We can't be friends. This last day proves that. And if we ever run into one another, accidentally or otherwise, we smile, say hello and go on our way. Agreed?'

'Isabella…'

'Agreed?'

Rowan nodded, looked at the ground and she swept out of the room, as elegantly as she could on knees that had turned to water.

Rowan reached for the handle of his suitcase but his hand only caught the air. When his focus returned, he grabbed for it and tugged. He had to get out of there. Away. He couldn't get back to his apartment in New York fast enough.

The problem was a journalist and a photographer blocking his exit from the room.

How fitting.

His heart rate was practically through the extra-high ceiling of the palace room but he put his head down and pulled on his case. Webber and the photographer stepped towards one another, actively sealing off his escape.

'You know she's right, don't you?'

Yes, he did, which was why he wanted to leave. Immediately.

'Which part in particular are you talking about?' Rowan said with a sigh.

They both laughed.

Both men were older. Both had worn-looking rings on the third finger of their left hands.

'The part about some random photographs not being the most important thing in the world?'

The part about her father.

The part about her family.

The part about him being a coward.

She was right about almost everything.

'I have a family to protect as well. That's why I did this.'

'Really?' asked Webber.

Rowan shook his head. 'You can hardly think I'm going to open up to you.'

'Why not? The interview ended when we said it did. We're not going to publish anything about her outburst just now, or whatever you might say now, without your permission.'

Rowan raised an eyebrow.

'We're not the bad guys you think we are. We do adhere to a code of ethics.'

'Excuse me if I don't believe you. I had to call off my wedding because of the things your colleagues did.'

'Not all journalists ignore professional ethics. And despite what you think, we are rarely trying to destroy people's lives.'

'No, that's just a bonus,' Rowan said.

It was snarky and the men could have been offended, but they smiled.

'The public have a desire to know about public figures, an insatiable need. I agree, there are bad eggs in our profession, but people do have a right to know certain things. There are things you want to know about public figures, aren't there? Politicians, leaders, business people?' Webber said and Rowan couldn't argue.

The press were important. But did they have to care so much about him and Isabella?

'Whether you wanted to be or not, you are a public figure. You have a public platform. You're a person the world wants to know about. And when you're with a woman who is universally beloved, especially when you hurt her, the world wants to know. They want to know if you're good enough for her.'

'Which I'm clearly not.'

Rowan wasn't sure where the words came from. The two men exchanged glances.

Great. So much for controlling the narrative.

This whole interview was meant to bury the last photo they didn't want released. And now one thing had led to another. And then another. And now he was spilling his guts to the enemy.

But Richard Webber and Thommy Spencer didn't look like the enemy, they just looked like two regular guys trying to do their job. Rowan sat in the nearest chair.

'It will never end, will it?' Rowan asked.

Spencer, the photographer, shook his head. 'You're famous, you always will be. But someone else more famous always comes along.'

'But how do I live like this? How can I change it?'

'A wise person once said, you can't always

change the world, but sometimes you can change what or how you think about it.'

Him. He'd said that. Not thirty minutes ago.

'You can't protect your loved ones…you can't stop bad things happening. But you can be with them if they do. I think that's what she was saying.'

Rowan clenched his teeth. He didn't need this man—this stranger—to tell him what Isabella was trying to say.

Except he did. Because he hadn't really been listening to anything Isabella had been saying lately. He'd listened to her words, but not the real meaning behind them. He hadn't seen her pain, he'd only heard what he'd wanted to hear, that she was fine, happy even, when really she was only pretending to be. For everyone's sake. Especially his.

Rowan looked at the men and didn't see a journalist or a photographer but two men he wouldn't mind going for a pint with.

'What am I going to do?' Rowan asked.

'I'd probably start with grovelling. And if that doesn't work, some sort of grand gesture. And maybe more grovelling,' Webber suggested.

Rowan didn't have time for a grand gesture. He didn't have time at all. He had a very small window before Isabella called palace security to throw him out of the place for good.

He didn't even have time to think about what he was going to say.

CHAPTER ELEVEN

JUST AS ISABELLA had known she would be, Francesca was waiting when Isabella returned to her rooms.

'So?'

'So…' Isabella flopped onto the nearest sofa and kicked off her shoes. 'I really need a bath.'

'You can have one in a minute, after you tell me how it went.'

'It went fine—'

'Great!'

'To begin with. And then it was an unmitigated disaster. I yelled at Rowan in front of the journalists, told him he'd broken my heart and made him promise never to speak to me again.'

Francesca's jaw dropped. 'Oh.'

'Oh, no, is more like it.'

'I'm sure…' Francesca began and then moved quickly around the room. 'Maybe we get the communications team to speak to them, reach some sort of understanding? Maybe you could speak to them again?'

Isabella shook her head. 'No. I'm done with this. I'm done trying to smooth this over, to hide my pain, to pretend everything is fine. I'm tired, Frannie. But most of all, I don't care if they think I'm heartbroken. I didn't say anything that wasn't the truth. I'm sick of putting on a perfect facade.' She tugged at the elastic holding her hair back and rubbed her scalp with her fingertips, fluffing out her hair. 'I don't care what they think of me anymore.'

As she spoke the words she was hit by their truth.

She didn't care. It was how she felt. And they were natural feelings. And justifiable. She didn't have to pretend. She had loved Rowan and he'd hurt her, let her down, and she wasn't afraid to say it.

'I'm sorry if that makes things difficult for you, and Mum and Dad, but I'm sick of being perfect.'

Francesca studied her sister. 'What brought this on?'

'Thirty years in the spotlight?'

Francesca smiled. 'I mean, you're different.'

Isabella opened her mouth to contradict her sister. She was the same person she'd always been except…she did feel different. She wasn't falling apart, she wasn't on the verge of tears, even though she'd just messed up the interview she'd been focusing on for the past week.

No. She felt together.

She felt strong for the first time in months. Even though she'd ruined the interview and she knew there would be fallout, she'd told Rowan how she really felt.

She'd been brave.

'You have a choice you know.'

'What do you mean?'

'You can choose your destiny.'

Isabella shook her head. 'I'll always be a princess.'

'I'm not saying you can choose who you are, because you're right, you can't, but you can change what you do and how you live. You don't have to stay here, you know, in Monterossa.'

'Are you trying to get rid of me?' Isabella joked, but her sister's words made sense.

'Not at all. I'm only saying that you have the skills and the qualifications to do so many things. And now you've told Rowan how you really feel, maybe you're ready, for not just a change, but also a challenge.'

She had wanted a change, for a while, but a change would mean leaving Francesca. Leaving Monterossa.

'I don't know if I could leave.'

'Not for ever, or anything like that. Maybe we've been selfish wanting to keep you here.'

'You haven't been keeping me here. I've been keeping myself here.'

Francesca nodded. She understood. The ties

that bound Isabella to Monterossa were loyalty and love only.

'You love Paris. And London. They aren't very far away.'

'I do feel ready for a change.' She'd once thought that marrying Rowan would be that change, but since that wasn't going to happen, it was up to her. 'I... I really could go anywhere. Do anything!'

You know what you want to do. You've known since your father got sick.

Francesca's face lit up, mirroring the joy that Isabella suddenly felt.

She wasn't stuck. She was free.

'I won't be gone for ever. I'm not abandoning you.'

'I know you're not. But soon it might be time for me to start the next part of my life, and it's time for you to as well. I might want you by my side always, but it would be selfish of me to insist on it. You need to build a life that doesn't revolve around me.'

'But I love you.'

'And I love you. And I will still love you, no matter where in the world you are.'

Isabella wondered if there was something else her sister wasn't telling her. Something she wasn't yet ready to. But either way, it didn't matter.

'Are you sure?'

Francesca laughed. 'I'd miss you, but of course

I'm sure. I've never expected you to shadow me for my entire life. I could not have asked for a more dedicated sister.'

'No.'

'It's not as though we'll never see one another. We'll talk every day. But you have a whole new adventure to have and you have to go and have it.'

So many possibilities suddenly presented themselves. She knew she wanted to learn more about skin cancer, but also to make sure others knew what she did.

'I love Monterossa.'

Francesca laughed. 'I know you do, but the world, literally, is your oyster.'

'Oysters? Yuck. Why can't it be my chocolate cake?'

'It can be whatever you want. The world can be whatever you want.'

Isabella went to her bathroom and turned on the bath. She had so many things to think about. She only had an idea, but now she realised she had time. And freedom. And she couldn't wait to get to work. The room quickly filled with steam and the noise of the running water and the thought of submerging herself in the tub already began to soothe her. She unbuttoned her skirt as she walked back into her bedroom. The door to her living area clicked and she called to her sister. 'Frannie? What's up?'

'I had to talk to you,' said a voice that was most definitely not her sister's.

'What are you doing here?' Isabella pulled her skirt around her and tried to button it back up. A task that was made harder with trembling hands. 'I said I didn't ever want to see you again.'

'I haven't left yet.'

'Clearly.'

Couldn't he get the message? She couldn't have made it clearer. We. Can't. See. One. Another. Ever. Again.

'I just had to tell you that you were right,' he said.

'I know I was right, which is why I told you I never wanted to see you again.' Because each time she did she felt her newfound resolve wavering. Something rose up inside her and pushed her to him.

'Yes, but that wasn't the part you were right about. I hope you'll agree you got that part very wrong. You were right that I should have been braver. Stronger. I shouldn't have hidden behind my family. I shouldn't have used them as an excuse.'

She knew it! He had been using his family and the media as an excuse all along. But for what?

'And what is the truth, Rowan?' Her voice shook and her body braced itself for fresh heartbreak.

That you don't love me enough?

'That I was scared I wasn't good enough for you.'

Oh.

She wanted to say, 'But that's ridiculous' and yet…

I'm sorry I wasn't strong enough.

She swallowed and thought back to London and the comments she'd brushed aside.

'Why would you doubt yourself?' she asked.

'Isabella, you're a princess.'

'So? That's a birthright, not an achievement.'

'I flunked out of school…'

'And then you developed a super-successful business that helps millions of people.'

'That was luck.'

'No, it wasn't. It was brilliance.'

'I listened to the haters. I'm sorry I did, and I will be sorry for ever for hurting you. You hid it so well, and I didn't question it. I wanted to believe that you were okay because it made things easier for me.'

Wow.

Isabella nodded. She understood, because she also understood that it wasn't always possible to be brave. It was often easier to push your feelings down and take the simplest path.

'Thank you for admitting that. It took courage.'

He laughed nervously. 'Hopefully next time my courage will be better timed. I don't know how to say this, and I don't have time to do anything grand because I suspect if I don't tell you this soon you'll have me thrown out of the palace. In fact, there's a good chance you'll have me thrown out anyway.'

'I don't know what you're saying.'

'I'm saying I love you. I love you and I never stopped loving you.'

She shook her head.

'It's true.'

'Why tell me this?' Why now? Nothing had changed with this revelation and the longer he stood in her bedroom, the harder he was making things.

'I had a chat with Richard and Thommy.'

'You spoke to the press?'

'Off the record.'

'Off the record! You know as well as I do that there's no such thing.'

'Maybe. But I trust them.'

As Isabella breathed in she shuddered. 'We went to all this trouble...'

'Yes, we did. And I hate to point it out, but you did go a little off script earlier as well.'

She couldn't meet his eye but could hear the smile in his voice. Her cheeks were on fire.

'You hurt me. A lot. I don't know if I can trust you again.' There, that was also the truth and hard to admit. Even though she longed for him, she couldn't just go back. She wasn't the woman she had been a year ago.

You aren't even the woman you were an hour ago.

'I thought you didn't care,' he whispered and then he was standing next to her, his feet beneath her gaze.

'I had to say that. I had to pretend it was all okay.'

'But it wasn't, was it? And I thought... I told myself that it was okay I wasn't strong enough because you didn't really mind.'

'Of course I minded! I love you and you broke my heart!'

Rowan took a step back. 'I'm sorry I didn't see it earlier.'

'You weren't meant to see it. I was pretending to be strong. I was pretending I was okay. I couldn't stand the idea of the world seeing how hurt I was.'

'I know, and I'm sorry you had to do that. I'm sorry about everything.'

She nodded, 'Thank you for saying that. But it's okay. And I meant what I said. I can't keep doing this. You need to leave.'

'Did you hear what I said earlier? The part about me loving you? And never stopping?'

She'd heard it, but it was words only. She'd never doubted his affection, only his commitment.

'But what's different? You still want to protect

your family. I'm still a princess. Neither of those things will ever change.'

'No. But maybe I have. I realised something in London: bad things will happen, I can't run away from them. I can only get through them. And it's always easier to get through things with you.'

She smiled, and her chest filled with warmth and love.

'I thought the same thing. As stressful as that night was, I almost didn't mind, because I was with you.'

Without knowing who moved first, she was in his arms, her cheek pressed against the warmth of his chest, his heartbeat reverberating around her.

She looked up into his golden eyes and found him staring down at her, smiling and enveloping her in his love.

Isabella lifted her feet and brought her lips the last few inches home. Home to Rowan.

His mouth opened to welcome her, caressing, kissing, confirming with each kiss how much he loved her. She fell deeper and deeper into the kiss, letting his embrace and his love surround her.

It couldn't be this simple, could it? Isabella shook herself and took a breath.

'Rowan, this is lovely, but I meant what I said. I can't play games anymore.'

'I know that.'

'So…' *Be brave. Ask for what you want. Ask*

for what you need. 'It's all or nothing, Rowan, I meant what I said before.'

He took her face gently into his strong hands. 'Isabella, I am asking for all. I love you enough to risk your parents' anger. I love you enough to stand up in front of the world and tell them I made a horrible mistake. Isabella, most of all, I even love you enough to knock on Francesca's door right now and tell her that I want you back.'

Isabella pressed her lips together, holding back a laugh.

'And that I want to marry you.'

Isabella closed her eyes and her stomach clenched. Images flashed across her mind, of her wedding dress, of Rowan's face when he told her he couldn't marry her, of the way none of the palace staff could meet her eyes for at least a month...

He stroked her cheek gently with his thumb. 'But you don't have to say anything about that now, and we don't have to make any decisions until you're ready. I need you to know that, no matter what, I'm in this for ever. If you tell me to leave, I will. But if you tell me to stay, I'll stay for ever.'

She looked at him, his eyes hopeful and full, just like her heart.

If he could be brave, she could as well.

'Stay,' she said, and he pulled her into his arms.

EPILOGUE

ISABELLA HAD OFFERED Rowan the option of an elopement, or a quiet wedding, but he'd refused. If she was comfortable then he would meet her at the end of the main aisle of the cathedral in Monterossa, just as they had planned last time.

The idea gave her family pause, but Isabella knew it was the right thing to do and this morning she'd been proven right, when she'd walked through the main arch of the cathedral just before eleven a.m.

Unlike last time, the wedding was in December, though in Southern Italy that was hardly cold. Isabella had worn a new ivory silk gown by a young, unknown designer, with several dozen tiny buttons up its back. She turned her back to Rowan now. 'I thought you might want to do me the honour of unbuttoning my dress.'

'You thought correctly. Though…' Rowan spun her back to face him. 'I would just like to look at you in this dress a little longer.'

She laughed. 'Really? I can't wait to get out of it.'

'And let me guess, into a bath?'

She smiled. 'No. Not just now.' Even though it had been a long day and the lead-up to the wedding had been intense, she didn't feel wrung out. She felt calm, centred. 'I meant I can't wait for both of us to get out of our clothes.'

Rowan's face expanded into a knowing smile. 'I see. But there's time for that. I would just like to admire my beautiful wife in her wedding gown for a few more moments.'

Isabella felt herself melting, as she often did, under his loving gaze. It was hard to believe she'd ever doubted his feelings for her, when everything he did and said confirmed how much he loved her. Day after day.

'You always look beautiful.'

'But?'

He grinned. 'But this will be the last time I see you in a wedding dress and I want to savour it.'

'I see you in a suit all the time, so I'm happy for you to take it off.' She grinned.

The lead-up to the wedding had gone smoothly. There had been negative publicity, of course— after all, this was the second wedding they had planned—and 'Will they? Won't they?' and 'Second time lucky!' were some of the less egregious headlines that had come out. But they both saw the headlines for what they were—click bait and an attempt to sell newspapers. Only they both knew the truth, which was that they were undeniably, irrevocably in love with one another and committed to each other for ever.

After a short honeymoon in Sicily, they would return to their new home in New York. Rowan would continue to work on his business and Isabella would return to her work at the Monterossan Embassy. In addition to that work, she was also working with Rowan on a secret project. Francesca joked that their 'secret project' was baby-making, but in truth it was developing a new application to monitor skin health. They were still working on the details, but it would involve a person tracking moles and skin irregularities over time to see if there were worrying changes. The work had made Isabella feel more energised and useful than she ever had in her life.

She was also in almost constant contact with Francesca, messaging each other at all hours of the day.

And when they were in Monterossa, which they planned to visit regularly, they had a new suite of rooms, where they were now. Still in the palace, but in a different wing, separate from the others. It would be their second home, their own space whenever they visited. It had several bedrooms in case their family grew and a balcony with a view over the sea.

She opened the French doors and walked out

to the balcony now. Rowan followed her and wrapped his arms around her and she leant into him.

'Did you see the papers?' she asked. Isabella hadn't picked up her phone since the night before.

'No, I'll leave that up to the communications team to deal with, but I'm sure it will be fine.'

Richard Webber and Thommy Spencer had been sent back to Monterossa to cover the event and they had given their only exclusive interview to them. They trusted them, especially after the lovely article they had first written about the pair of them. Webber had been true to his word and the piece had been honest but without any mention of the off-the-record confrontation he and Thommy had witnessed. The article had also been particularly complimentary about Rowan's new app, which had become one of the biggest selling of all time within the first week of its launch.

'I'm not going to give a single thought to the rest of the world and what they're saying about anything for at least...'

'A night? A week?'

He laughed. 'I was going to say for ever.'

They smiled as Rowan pulled Isabella into his arms and they looked together over the sea and the setting sun.

* * * * *

*Look out for the next story in
the Princesses' Night Out duet*
Temptation in a Tiara *by Karin Baine*

*And if you enjoyed this story,
check out these other great reads
from Justine Lewis*

Swipe Right for Mr. Perfect
The Billionaire's Plus-One Deal
Breaking the Best Friend Rule

All available now!